THE BOBBSEY TWINS'
MYSTERY OF THE KING'S PUPPET

"It's a ghost!" cries Flossie Bobbsey. But when the lights are turned on, the twins see a big puppet—a knight in shining armor. It belongs to the Bobbseys' Italian friend, Dom Amato, whom they are visiting in New York. Next morning the boy and his puppet have vanished. The Bobbseys fly to Italy to search for him, and the exciting chase leads to the island of Sicily.

There is more than one puzzle to solve. Why has Dom been kidnapped? Why did Grandfather Martino pay a midnight visit to the woodcarver? And who is the Mystery Cat, the prankster who plays such funny tricks in Palermo? Readers will thrill as the Bobbseys unravel the mysteries and succeed in making two families very happy.

THE BOBBSEY TWINS BOOKS
By Laura Lee Hope

"Watch out!" Bert shouted

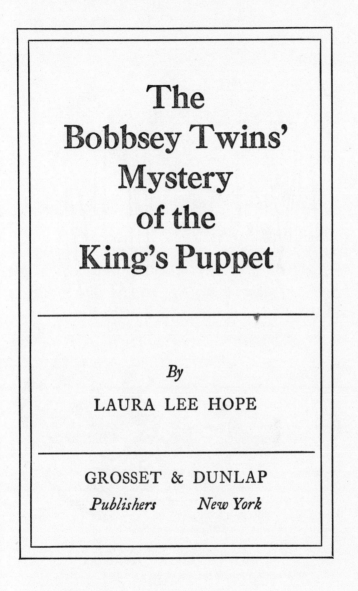

The
Bobbsey Twins' Mystery of the King's Puppet

By

LAURA LEE HOPE

GROSSET & DUNLAP
Publishers   *New York*

COPYRIGHT © 1967 BY GROSSET & DUNLAP, INC.
PUBLISHED SIMULTANEOUSLY IN CANADA
ALL RIGHTS RESERVED

PRINTED IN THE UNITED STATES OF AMERICA
LIBRARY OF CONGRESS CATALOGUE CARD NUMBER: 67–13652
The Bobbsey Twins' Mystery of the King's Puppet

CONTENTS

CHAPTER I

FLOSSIE SEES A GHOST

"WHY is that man staring at us?" whispered blond, blue-eyed Flossie Bobbsey. She nodded toward a large, bald-headed man peering in the window of the New York ice cream shop.

"Maybe he's looking for someone," her twelve-year-old brother Bert replied.

"Nobody's here tonight but us," said Nan, his dark-haired twin, as she looked around the large, cool shop. Her parents were seated at a table in the rear talking to the owner.

"Ummm, this Italian ice cream is yummy!" exclaimed Freddie, who was Flossie's twin. They were six. Freddie dug his spoon into the large rainbow-colored slice on his plate.

Just then the door burst open and the big man stepped inside. He strode toward the children's table and snatched up Bert's dish of ice cream. As the boy grabbed it, the whole thing fell upside down on Bert's head!

With a gasp he jumped up. Ice cream was running down his face. "What's the idea?" he demanded.

By this time the owner, a small man, was dashing forward, his plump face red with anger.

"Stop! Stop!" he cried.

Mr. and Mrs. Bobbsey followed him in astonishment. The children stared, amazed.

"Sorry," the big man said. "I just wanted to put some in a bottle. It was an accident!"

"Accident nothing!" exclaimed the little proprietor. "You've gone too far!" He reached up and waggled a finger in the man's face. "Get out and don't come back!"

The big fellow gave a mean laugh. "There'll be plenty more accidents around here," he growled, "unless you sell me what I want!" He turned and left the shop, slamming the door behind him.

"Let's chase him!" cried Freddie. "He can't do that to my brother!"

He and Nan dashed outside. In the light of a street lamp they saw the man climb into a black car and drive off.

"Oh shucks!" said Freddie.

When the children returned, the others were helping Bert wipe his head with paper napkins. Mr. Amato, the proprietor, hurried to a curtained doorway at the rear of the shop. "Dom!" he called. "Bring towels!"

In a few moments a tall boy wearing a white apron came in. He was about fifteen and had broad shoulders and dark curly hair like the shop owner. He looked in surprise at Bert.

Mr. Amato took the towels from him and said, "Dom, this is Bert Bobbsey. Take him to the kitchen and help him wash off the ice cream."

"Okay, Uncle Mario." Dom grinned. "Come on, Bert."

Mr. Amato turned to the twins' parents. "Richard—Mary! I am so sorry! To have such a terrible thing happen in my shop!"

"It wasn't your fault, Mario," said Mrs. Bobbsey kindly. She was a slender, pretty woman. "Who is that awful man and what did he mean he was going to put some of the ice cream in a bottle?"

"His name is Carlo Vito," the proprietor replied, as he began to wipe the table with one of the towels. Nan took the other and helped as he went on talking.

"I have known Vito since we were boys in Sicily. He's a bully—always has been. A month ago he came here to New York for a visit. For a week Vito has been threatening me. Tonight he embarrasses me! It is because he is trying to make me sell the special recipe I use for my ice cream. Naturally I won't do it."

"Why not?" asked Freddie.

"Because the recipe is very valuable," Mr.

Amato said, putting aside the towel and sitting down. "It took a long time to perfect it. Vito thought he would take some away tonight and have it analyzed so he could learn my secret.

"For almost a hundred years the Amato family has made ice cream in Sicily, where I was born. Everyone there knows how good it is." He looked scornful. "Now Vito wants to open a chain of ice cream shops in Sicily using my name and selling my ice cream."

The little man's face grew pink again. "I know him! He'd make the ice cream so poorly that he would bring shame to our reputation." Mr. Amato thumped his fist on the table. "Never will I sell to him!"

"It's delicious ice cream," Nan said soothingly. "I love the teeny bits of chocolate and fruit in it."

Mr. Amato smiled at her. "There's something else, too," he whispered. "A special ingredient—that's what makes it so good. You know," he added proudly, "I not only have this shop, but I sell to all the fine restaurants and hotels in New York."

"Can't you tell the police about the bad man?" Flossie asked.

"You don't know Carlo Vito," said the ice cream maker. "He's a fast worker. He can do plenty of damage before the police catch up with him."

Mr. Amato leaned toward the children's parents. "I am especially worried because of the you-know-what for the you-know-who." He rolled his eyes toward the children.

Mr. Bobbsey, a tall, youthful-looking man, nodded gravely. The twins smiled. Mr. Amato and their parents had a surprise for them! Was it something they were going to do in New York?

The Bobbsey family had come from their home in Lakeport the day before to spend two weeks in the big city. Now an exciting thing was going to happen! The children could tell.

Mrs. Bobbsey changed the subject at once. "Tell us why you decided to bring your ice cream business to America," she said to Mr. Amato. The shop owner told her that when he grew up he and his brother were the only two members of the family left.

"Guiseppe did not like to make ice cream," said Mr. Amato, "and I wanted to live in America. So I brought the recipe over and opened my shop here on Mulberry Street."

Mr. Amato noticed that Nan and Freddie had finished eating their ice cream. He went to the counter, placed a slice in a dish and gave it to Nan. "Take this to your brother. He and Dom are in our apartment behind the shop. The kitchen's at the end of the hall."

Nan thanked him. She and Freddie went through the flowered curtains. A few minutes later

Flossie finished eating, pushed back her chair, and followed them. She found herself alone in a long narrow hallway, dimly lit by a wall lamp.

"Oo, it's spooky," Flossie thought.

She started walking and passed a closed door on her left. The next one was partly open. As she reached it, the little girl stopped short. *What was that funny noise?* A light clanking sound was coming from inside the room.

"Maybe Freddie is playing a trick on me," she thought, and called him. There was no answer. "Who's in there?" Flossie asked, her voice trembling. The clanking sound came again.

The little girl peered into the unlit room and gasped. In one corner she saw a light figure floating in the air!

"It's a ghost!" she exclaimed.

Flossie raced to the end of the hall and burst into the kitchen. Bert and the others looked up in surprise as Flossie cried, "I saw a ghost!"

"Where?" asked Freddie.

"In that second room," said Flossie. "I heard him clanking around!"

Dom grinned and stood up. "That's my room," he said. "Come and meet your ghost."

Flossie took Nan's hand and followed the others. Dom led the way to the open door and reached inside to flick on the light.

"Oh!" exclaimed Nan as the others gasped.

Hanging from a hook in the ceiling was the

"It's a ghost!"

biggest and most beautiful puppet they had ever seen! He was dressed in dark metal armor with a great red plume in his helmet. As a breeze came through the open window he swung lightly and his armored legs clanked together.

"He's bee-yoo-ti-ful!" Flossie exclaimed. "What's his name?"

"Orlando," Dom replied. "Back home in Sicily, there are lots like him."

Dom explained that long ago the Emperor Charlemagne had a company of brave knights who were called paladins. "Orlando was his favorite," said Dom. "He is the hero of many stories played by the puppet theaters in Sicily."

"I have never seen such a big puppet," said Nan. "It must have very strong strings."

"Orlando works on rods," said Dom. He pulled a chair across the room, climbed up and pointed out where the man working him, the puppeteer, could attach rods at the top of the head and on the arms.

"There's a hole in Orlando's hand," said Freddie.

"That's where his iron sword is supposed to be bolted," Dom told him. "But now he doesn't have the sword or any rods."

"Did you bring him from Sicily?" Flossie asked.

"No. I found him right here in a Greenwich Village antique shop. I didn't have to pay much for him either!" Dom patted the knight's shoulder.

Nan walked up and shook Orlando's hand. "How do you do, Orlando." Each of the other twins did the same.

"This is a keen room," said Bert, looking around at the colored pictures of puppets on the walls.

Over the desk was a large map of Italy with the island of Sicily just off the end of it.

Dom pointed to a dot on the northern shore with a red circle drawn around it. "That's my home—Palermo. It's Orlando's, too." Dom's eyes lighted happily. "I was very lucky to find him. He's a special puppet, you see."

"What do you mean?" Bert asked.

"There's a secret about Orlando," said Dom. Just then Mr. Amato called from the shop. "Dom! Customers!"

"Sorry," the boy said. "I have to go." He hurried out.

Bert and the girls began to examine the pictures on the walls, but Freddie climbed onto the chair beside the puppet. As he stood on tiptoe to feel the knight's plume, he teetered forward. "Help!" the little boy cried and grabbed the puppet for support.

Crash! Down tumbled the armored figure with Freddie on top of it. The others came running.

"Freddie, are you hurt?" Nan cried.

Freddie sat up. "I'm okay," he said.

Suddenly Nan gasped in horror and pointed upward. The puppet's helmeted head still swung from the ceiling!

CHAPTER II

THE ROYAL KNIGHT

FREDDIE scrambled to his feet and looked down at the puppet's headless body. "I didn't mean to hurt it," he said.

Just then Dom burst in. "What happened?" He saw the armored body on the floor. "I thought so. I heard a crash."

Freddie's lip quivered, but he stepped forward. "I did it," he said. "I'm sorry."

"Can the puppet be fixed?" asked Bert.

Dom laughed. "He's not broken."

Flossie's eyes grew wide. "But his head's off!"

"It's supposed to come off," said Dom.

"You mean it?" exclaimed Freddie. He heaved a sigh of relief and sat down on Dom's bed.

"Sure. These knights play lots of battle scenes," said Dom, "so they often have their heads cut off." He drew an imaginary sword and leaped forward. "Like this!" he cried, with a swoop of his arm. "And whoosh! Off comes the head!"

11

"Oh, that's great!" said Bert.

"It's not so easy to do," said Dom. "Just as one operator makes a puppet slash with his sword, the other puppeteer has to push down on his knight's head rod and twist it. That unhooks the head from a loop on top of the body." He glanced up at the head, where a metal loop dangled from a hook. "I knew that loop was loose. When Freddie grabbed the body, his added weight pulled it out."

"He shouldn't have been touching the puppet," Bert said, with a stern look at his brother.

Dom stepped onto the chair and lifted down the wooden head. "Somebody get the glue from the desk," he said.

Freddie ran over and brought back the bottle. Dom set the heavy body on the bed, then squeezed some of the sticky fluid into the hole in the wood where the loop had been.

"Is that Orlando's secret—that his head comes off?" Flossie asked.

"No. I don't know the secret," Dom replied as he took the loop and fitted it into the gluey hole. "Nobody knows—not even the Martinos."

"Who are they?" Nan asked.

"They own the puppet theater across the street from my house in Palermo," Dom replied. "Papa Martino and his three sons put on the paladin plays. This Orlando belongs to them."

He explained that Grandfather Martino had

told his family there was a secret about the marionette, but he had died before revealing it. Dom went on to say that several years ago the puppet had been stolen from the theater. "The Martinos have never stopped looking for Orlando and hoping to get him back."

"Have you told them that you found him?" Bert asked.

"No," Dom replied. "I just discovered him day before yesterday."

"Won't the Martinos be thrilled when they hear!" Nan exclaimed.

"Are you going to send Orlando home soon?" Freddie asked.

Dom did not answer Freddie's question, but told them how he had spotted the puppet in the shopwindow. "It was a lucky accident," he said.

"How do you think the puppet got to this country?" Nan asked.

Dom shrugged. "Probably the thief sold it to a tourist who brought it to New York. I guess the person sold it to the antique dealer."

Bert looked closely at the figure. "How can you be sure this is the same puppet that was stolen?" he asked.

"By the armor. It's real silver. Also," Dom added, "there's this." He pointed to a small dent in the shield the knight held in one hand. "I was always playing around the theater and saw Orlando up close many times. Besides he is very old." As the boy carefully hooked the puppet's head to the loop, he showed them tiny cracks in the painted face. "This fellow only played holiday performances. There is an everyday Orlando who does the part most of the time."

"Why is this one so special?" Nan asked.

"Because he is the King's Puppet," Dom told her.

The twins' eyes sparkled with interest. "What king?" asked Flossie.

"The first king of Italy," Dom replied. "You see, when Italy became a nation there was a great celebration in Rome. Great-grandfather Martino took his family there to give a command performance with the puppets. His Majesty was so pleased with it that he had this marionette especially made for the Martinos."

"Then Orlando really and truly is a royal knight," Nan said.

Bert looked puzzled. "Is he a marionette or a puppet, Dom?"

The boy smiled. "Both. A marionette is a puppet that works on strings or rods."

"What are those called?" asked Flossie, pointing to a row of soda bottles on Dom's desk. Propped on top of each was a funny head with a cloth skirt.

"Hand puppets," said Dom. He quickly fitted a mouse over one hand and a lion over the other.

Then from the big boy's lips came a tiny voice:

"How about a piece of cheese for lunch?" The mouse cocked its head.

The lion shook his mane. "You'd better get out before I eat *you* for lunch!" he roared.

Flossie giggled and Freddie cried, "May I try it—please?"

"Sure," said Dom. "Go ahead." He tossed the puppets to the young twins.

Nan ran a finger over Orlando's shield. "Too bad his armor isn't shiny."

"It used to be when the Martinos had him," Dom replied, "but now it's tarnished. I want to polish it."

"We'll help you," said Nan. "Have you any silver polish?"

With a quick nod Dom hurried away and soon returned with damp sponges, clean rags, and a jar of pink polishing cream. While Freddie and Flossie played lion and mouse with the hand puppets, roaring and squeaking at each other, Bert, Nan, and Dom began to work on the silver armor. After they had rubbed for a while, small shining patches appeared.

"It'll be a big job," said Nan with a sigh. "We'll come back in the morning and do some more if you want us to."

Before Dom could answer, Freddie put down his lion and said, "Why did you come to America, Dom?"

The boy told the Bobbseys that his father, Mr.

Amato's brother Guiseppe, had died the year before. "Uncle Mario has no family except Della, his daughter. So he wanted me to come to New York and learn the ice cream business."

"Is it fun making ice cream?" Flossie asked.

"Not for me," said Dom. "I'd rather be a puppeteer."

"Don't you like it here?" Nan asked.

"Oh, Uncle Mario's nice to me," said Dom, "and Della is lots of fun." He explained that his cousin, who was eighteen, was out to a party. "But I miss home and Italy and the puppet theater. Besides," he added, "my mother wrote me that mysterious things are going on in our neighborhood."

The Bobbseys looked interested. "We like to solve mysteries," said Nan. "Too bad we aren't in Italy now. We were in Venice a little while ago."

Before she could say more, a cheerful whistle sounded from the shop. "That's Daddy," said Flossie. "We have to go."

The children returned to the shop where all the Bobbseys said good night to Mr. Amato and his nephew.

As the family went out the door, Nan turned back. "Oh, I almost forgot," she said to Dom. "Do you want us to come tomorrow and polish Orlando?"

The boy hesitated, but Mr. Amato said, "Of

course he does! That's a fine idea! You come right along first thing in the morning!"

In the taxi on the way uptown to the hotel, Nan told her parents about the puppet, and Mrs. Bobbsey gave permission for the twins to go back to the shop.

Early the next day the children taxied to Mulberry Street. On the way it began to rain.

When they entered the store, it was empty. "Mr. Amato," Bert called, and a moment later the flowered curtains parted. A pretty, slender girl stood there. She had short black hair with bangs.

"I'm Della," she said. "You must be the Bobbseys. Please come in." Her large dark eyes were sad and she did not smile.

Della led them down the hall to Dom's room. On the bed sat Mr. Amato with his head sunk in his hands.

Before anyone could speak, Flossie pointed to the corner. "Orlando—he's gone!"

"And so is Dom," said Mr. Amato. He handed Nan a piece of paper. "Read this. Dom left it on his pillow."

Nan read the pencil-printed words aloud: "Dear Uncle Mario, I am sorry, but I just can't stay any longer. Thanks for everything and don't worry. Love, Dom."

As she handed it back to Mr. Amato, his eyes filled with tears.

"Poor Papa," said Della, putting her arm around her father. "He has no son to carry on the ice cream business and he was hoping Dom would do it."

"I taught him everything," said Mr. Amato sadly. "He knows how to make the ice cream and the special ingredient as well as I do."

"But his heart wasn't in it," Della said gently.

Bert spoke up. "Are you sure that's Dom's printing?"

"Yes. it's his," replied Della. "Why?"

"Maybe somebody made him write the note," said Bert, looking worried.

"You think he was kidnaped?" asked Nan.

"Oh no! Not that!" cried Mr. Amato. He grew pale and began to tremble. While the children tried to calm him, Nan thought she heard a board squeak in the hall. She nudged Bert. "I think there's someone out there," she whispered.

The two stepped quietly to the open door and checked the corridor. It was empty.

"Look!" said Nan. There was a wet print of a man's shoe beside the door. "He must have been standing here, listening."

As she spoke, Bert caught her arm and pointed toward the curtains at the end of the hall. They stirred slightly and they saw the toes of a pair of men's shoes. Bert gestured for Nan to follow and they tiptoed toward the hidden man.

"Grab him!" Bert cried

"Grab him!" cried Bert. The twins leaped upon the curtains and flung their arms around them. No one was there!

With a loud rip the material came down and the twins fell. Scrambling out from under the curtains, they heard the shop door slam.

"An eavesdropper!" exclaimed Bert as the others came running into the hall. "Quick! Everybody after him!"

The children and Della dashed out onto the sidewalk, but saw only a few women passing by.

They went back inside and found Mr. Amato sitting at one of the tables.

"Why should anyone be eavesdropping on us?" he asked.

"Perhaps the man who was listening knows something about Dom's disappearance and wants to find out what you're going to do."

Nan shook her head. "I don't think Dom was kidnapped." She told them how the boy had hesitated when she asked if they should come the next day. "I think Dom knew he would not be here."

"Where do you suppose he is, Mr. Amato?" asked Flossie.

"That's what I'd like to know!" came a loud voice. The surprised group looked up to see a large red-haired man in the doorway. "Dom Amato stole my puppet!"

CHAPTER III

A POTATO SURPRISE

EVERYONE stared at the stranger in surprise. Then Mr. Amato jumped to his feet. "You take that back!" he exclaimed. "My nephew never stole anything from anyone!"

"Who are you?" Della asked the stranger. "What's this all about?"

The man replied that he was Henry Wood, the owner of the antique shop where Dom had found the puppet. "My clerk says Dom Amato came in, examined the puppet, and then carried it out of the shop when he wasn't looking."

"I don't believe Dom did that," declared Bert, and the others agreed.

"How did your clerk know his name?" Nan asked.

The man pulled a postcard from his pocket and handed it to Della. "The boy dropped this."

Della looked at it and said, "Yes, this is Dom's —from his mother."

Bert frowned. "If the clerk thought Dom stole the puppet, why didn't he call the police right away?"

The man replied that the boy he had left in charge was young and inexperienced. "He waited to tell me about it and I just got back from a trip this morning."

Nan spoke up. "Dom said he paid for the puppet."

"Naturally, he said that," the man replied sourly. "Now where is he?"

"We don't know," said Mr. Amato. "He's gone and the puppet with him."

Mr. Wood's eyes narrowed. "Oh, is that so! Then I guess I'd better call the police." He started for the door.

"No wait!" cried Nan. "Please, Mr. Wood, let us try to find Dom!"

"I'm sure there's some mistake," put in Della. "As soon as we get in touch with him, it can be straightened out."

The man hesitated, looking at the pleading faces before him. "All right," he growled. "But I expect to hear from you by six o'clock tonight, or I'll file charges against the boy."

He turned on his heel and went out, shutting the door hard behind him.

The ice cream man sighed. "He means it, I'm afraid. We must find Dom. Where can he be?"

"Did he have any money?" Bert asked.

"Yes," said Mr. Amato. "He saved quite a lot from his salary."

"Then I bet he went home to Sicily," said Nan.

"We'd better check the airlines right away," Bert added.

"Boats, too," put in Freddie.

"Good idea," Mr. Amato agreed. "We have a phone here and one in the kitchen."

"And there's three in the drugstore on the corner," added Della.

"We'll list all the numbers and divide them up," said Bert. "Nan and I'll call from the drugstore."

Five minutes later when the lists were finished, Della hurried to the cash register and got out a handful of dimes. "Here, everybody, take some and let's go!"

The Bobbseys hastened down the street to the telephone booths and as the older twins called, the younger ones fed them the numbers and dimes.

Suddenly Bert burst from his booth. "Nan, you were right! I've found the airline Dom flew on."

The children ran back to the shop, where Della was dialing a number.

"He's gone to Palermo!" Bert shouted. Della hung up the phone and followed the children as they raced to the kitchen to tell Mr. Amato.

"I heard you!" cried the ice cream man. "When did he leave?"

"At midnight," said Bert.

"Would he be home yet?" asked Nan.

"No. He has to change planes at Rome and at Naples. Palermo is the last stop."

"As soon as he arrives," said Nan, "we can get in touch with him and find out about the puppet."

Mr. Amato looked worried. "But he might leave the plane in Naples. He's always wanted to see that city."

Della nodded. "And he might not go home for days!"

"That's terrible!" exclaimed Nan. "We must talk to Dom and report to Mr. Wood before six o'clock."

Bert looked at notes he had made in the telephone booth. "Dom's due to arrive in Naples any minute!" he said, then added, "You'd better call the airline right away, Della, and ask them to radio the authorities at the Naples airport to hold Dom there. Then Mr. Amato can talk to him on the transatlantic telephone and get his story."

Della called the airline and spoke to one of the officials. After hanging up, she reported that the man would let them know as soon as Dom had been picked up.

"They can't miss him," said Freddie, 'cause he'll be carrying that big puppet."

"I'm afraid that's not so," said Della. "Dom's duffel bag is the only other thing that's missing, so Orlando must be in it."

"Anyway," said Bert, "that bag will go in the baggage compartment."

Twenty minutes later when the phone rang, everybody jumped. Della answered eagerly. After she had listened a few moments, her face fell. She thanked the caller and hung up. "Dom has slipped through our fingers," she reported. "An officer picked him up as he left customs, but Dom managed to get away. The airline has asked the Naples police to look for him."

"Now what will you do?" asked Flossie.

"Close the store and go after him as soon as we can," said Mr. Amato firmly. "I can't just sit here while my nephew is in trouble."

"This spoils the you-know-what," said Della, glancing at the children.

"Oh, please tell us the surprise," begged Flossie.

Mr. Amato smiled. "It was a trip. Two weeks from today the Bobbseys and Amatos were going to Italy together."

"Oh, what a super idea!" said Nan as the other children exclaimed in delight.

Della smiled. "Papa and I could have shown you around. I've been there twice."

"But that's all off now," said Mr. Amato firmly. "Della and I must go at once to find Dom."

"If he sees us he might run away," she remarked. "We'll need eyes in back of our heads."

Bert and Nan exchanged excited looks.

"Mr. Amato," said Bert eagerly, "let us help!"

And Nan urged, "That would make four extra pairs of eyes."

"Oh yes," put in Freddie. "We'd find Dom for you!"

"And I'll bet he wouldn't run away from us!" added Flossie.

Mr. Amato stared at the twins a moment. "Your Daddy told me you were good detectives," he said. "It might not be a bad idea. What do you say, Della?"

"I'm *for* it!" she exclaimed.

"Oh, let's ask Mother and Daddy right away!" cried Flossie.

Mr. Amato called the hotel and the children listened breathlessly as he talked first to their mother and then their father. After listening awhile, he said good-by and hung up.

He smiled into their anxious faces. "All right. You're going."

Freddie whooped and turned a handspring as Della hugged Nan, and Flossie clapped her hands.

"Now I'd better cable Aunt Bartolina," said Della. "That's Dom's mother."

"Tell her Dom is on the way to Palermo and so are we, but we cannot say exactly when we'll arrive," said Mr. Amato.

"All right." Della turned to the twins. "I'll see about plane tickets and let you know when to be ready."

"What about Mr. Wood?" Bert asked.

"It's very unfair to accuse Dom of stealing," said Nan, "when he isn't here to defend himself."

"I'll go see Mr. Wood," the boy's uncle said, "and explain what we are doing. Maybe he'll be willing to wait and listen to Dom's story."

"Don't worry, Mr. Amato," said Flossie, patting his hand. "We'll find Dom."

The man smiled. "Call me Uncle Mario. I wish I had half a dozen children just like you."

Della laughed and told the twins to run along and pack. "We'll meet you in your hotel lobby."

The Amatos arrived that evening just as the airport limousine was announced. Mr. and Mrs. Bobbsey kissed and hugged all the children. "We'll meet you in Rome in two weeks," said their mother.

"What did Mr. Wood say?" Bert asked Mr. Amato.

"He will give us two weeks to find Dom. After that—he will make the story public."

Just then the hotel clerk called Bert over and handed him a square box wrapped in brown paper. "Sorry," he said. "This came today but was mislaid."

"Who's it from?" Freddie asked, as Bert returned.

"Danny Rugg," replied his brother, pointing to the scrawled return address.

Freddie groaned. Danny was a boy about Bert's age who often made trouble for the Bobbseys.

"When Danny heard we were going to New York, he said he would send us a present," Flossie reminded them.

"Let's open it on the plane," Nan said. "There's no time now."

Two hours later as the big jetliner soared over the ocean, Freddie tore off the string and paper. Flossie was next to him and Bert by the window. Nan watched from across the aisle where she sat with the Amatos.

"Take it easy," Bert warned. "It might be a trick."

As he spoke Freddie lifted the lid.

Z-Zing! Something flew from the box and back over their heads. The next moment there was a sharp outcry behind them.

Bert jumped up, and Freddie and Flossie quickly kneeled and looked over the back of the seat. There sat a large man with bushy black hair and a big mustache. Bouncing in his lap was a long spring with a silly plastic potato-head on the end of it.

Freddie gulped. "Oh, I'm sorry! It was a joke!"

The man's black eyes gleamed fiercely. "Joke?" he rumbled.

"On us, I mean," said Freddie weakly.

"Yes," Bert added and tried to explain.

Glowering, the man thrust the spring at Freddie, but said nothing. The children sat down again, red-faced.

Z-ZING! Something flew through the air!

"I'll get that Danny Rugg," Freddie muttered. "I'm going to think of a present to send him."

Before long the lights were turned out. "I want to stay awake," Flossie said, "and see the sun come up." But the next thing she knew, it was daylight and the stewardess was giving the children hot damp towels to wipe their hands and faces.

Next came a breakfast of juice and eggs and hot rolls. Afterward a voice on the loudspeaker announced that they were landing in Rome.

"Now remember," said Mr. Amato as they left the plane, "we have to wait here a couple of hours for our flight to Naples."

In the terminal Bert noticed the man who had been sitting behind them. He was wearing a wide-brimmed black hat now. Several times the boy caught the stranger looking at them over the top of his newspaper.

Later when they boarded the plane for Naples, the man was right behind them.

"Why is he so interested in us?" Bert wondered. But by the time the plane landed in Naples all the Bobbseys' thoughts were on Dom and the King's Puppet.

"Let's ask all the taxi drivers at the airport if they saw Dom," Nan suggested to Della as they left the plane. "You can teach us how to ask in Italian."

Freddie was the last one out. At the door the

man in the black hat tapped him on the shoulder.

"I'll bet you're going to the Coro Hotel, little boy," he said, smiling.

Freddie looked surprised. "I don't know the name. Mr. Amato says it's a big one on a hill."

The man smiled wider, pushed past and hurried away.

"I guess he's not mad at us any more," Freddie thought.

A little while later, the Bobbseys and their friends came out of the terminal with their baggage. Each of them went to a taxi and spoke to the driver in Italian. "Did you pick up a boy with a duffel bag yesterday?"

The third man Bert talked to had a long face and limp black hair. He stared as the boy spoke the strange words slowly. Then he nodded. "*Si.*"

Excited, Bert called the others, and they came running.

"This is the one!" he exclaimed.

"Get in, get in!" said Della quickly.

"Can we all fit?" asked Flossie, eyeing the taxi, which was smaller than those at home.

"Yes, go ahead," said Mr. Amato. "I'll follow in the next one."

The baggage was quickly loaded into the second cab, and the children piled in with Della. The taxi started with a lurch and shot out onto the road. Mr. Amato's cab came roaring close behind.

"Ask where he took Dom," Bert said to Della.

She leaned forward and spoke loudly to the driver. The man replied rapidly, waving his arm.

"What did he say?" Nan asked eagerly.

Della frowned. "He says he took Dom some place, but he won't tell where."

CHAPTER IV

A SINGING MESSAGE

THE children looked surprised. "Why won't he tell us where he took Dom?" Nan asked.

"I don't know," said Della. She spoke to the driver in Italian. He replied loudly, waving one hand. The children swayed as the taxi swerved!

"He says he promised Dom not to tell," Della reported. "This man ran away from home as a boy and he says he knows how Dom feels."

Another stream of Italian came from the front seat and the girl translated again. "He says he's been avoiding the police at the airport so he wouldn't have to answer their questions. Naturally, he won't answer ours either."

As the taxi zipped around a corner, Bert said, "We'd better not get him so excited while he's driving."

Suddenly the car lurched to a stop at a crossroad and a stream of traffic passed in front of it. Flossie touched the driver gently on the shoul-

der. He turned around and saw that her big blue
eyes were filled with tears.

"Please tell us where you took Dom," the little
girl pleaded. "His uncle and Della are so worried."

The man's dark eyes softened. He twitched his
nose and sighed. Then he turned back to the
wheel. As the taxi roared forward, he shouted
back at them.

Della grinned. "He promised not to *tell*, but
he'll *take* us to the street!"

The children beamed, and Freddie said, "Did
he understand Flossie?"

Della laughed. "No, but he couldn't bear to
see her cry."

When they reached the crowded city, the man
drove skillfully along the waterfront and soon
turned up a narrow, steep street. Lines of colored
clothes hung from one side to the other.

"It must be washday," Nan said.

Della laughed. "There are always lines of dry-
ing clothes hung across the old streets of Naples."

At the top of the hill, the cab stopped. The
one behind did, too. Everyone got out and Mr.
Amato asked his driver to wait, then paid the
man in the first cab. As it sped away, the driver
waved wildly at a house with a sign in the window.

"That says, 'Room for rent,'" said Della.

"I'll bet Dom went there," Bert remarked.

They walked to the door, where a woman in a
black dress was seated on the stoop. Mr. Amato

spoke to her in Italian. At her reply, he frowned.

"Dom stayed here last night," he said. "But he left this morning and she doesn't know where he went."

Mr. Amato suggested that the others go on to the hotel while he stopped to see if the police had word of the boy.

An hour later he met them in the lobby of their large, airy hotel on a hill above the city. The police had no news. "They're watching the airport," said Mr. Amato, "and will catch him as soon as he tries to use his plane ticket to Palermo."

"But Dom must know that," said Bert. "I'll bet he'll try to take a boat to Palermo."

"He can't have much money left," said Mr. Amato. "He'd have to work for his passage."

"Let's go to the waterfront and see what we can find out," Nan said eagerly.

Freddie spoke up. "Isn't it nearly dinner time? I'm starved."

Mr. Amato smiled and patted the little boy's shoulder. "We'll have something to eat there, Freddie. And then I'm going to take you to a place I know for a very special dessert."

Della laughed. "Wait until you see it—parasol cake!"

Freddie grinned. "Do we have to eat a parasol?"

"You'll find out," said Della.

Again they set off in two taxis which took

them to a row of restaurants and stores along the bay. On the other side of the wide, noisy street was a long line of docks.

The twins and their friends began to walk, and soon Mr. Amato pointed to a steamer. "That one goes to Palermo."

"Then Dom might have eaten in here," said Bert, stopping in front of a crowded open-front restaurant. "Let's find out."

When they had seated themselves at a marble-topped table and ordered spaghetti, Mr. Amato asked for the proprietor. He was directed to the back, where a thin, olive-skinned man was working hard behind a high counter. Uncle Mario questioned him, then returned to the table, his face pink with excitement. "You were right, Bert!" he exclaimed. "Dom tried to get a job on the steamer this morning, but there were no openings. Then he came here and asked the owner if he knew of any other boat going to Palermo."

While he spoke a handsome, dark-haired man with a guitar had been leaning against a post and singing Italian songs to the customers. Now he bent close to them and sang, "Ask me about the boy."

"He's singing a message!" Flossie exclaimed.

The man smiled and stopped playing. Speaking in broken English, he told them that he had seen the boy outside the restaurant talking to a tall,

"He's singing a message!" Flossie exclaimed

thin man in a red-striped shirt. They had gone off together.

"Did you hear what they said?" Bert asked.

The man shook his head. "Only something about 'the purple fish.'"

"The purple fish!" Nan exclaimed. "What did he mean?"

The man shrugged. "But I know the tall fellow. He is Ricco Tucci—a sneak thief."

The travelers exchanged worried looks. Bert suggested that they leave a message for the boy with the singer.

The musician agreed. "I sing in all the waterfront restaurants. I may see him again."

Bert gave the singer their hotel address and asked him to tell Dom to get in touch with the Bobbseys. Meanwhile Nan left their address with the restaurant owner and asked him to call if he saw the boy.

After eating, Uncle Mario led the way up a side street and into a sweet shop.

"I see the parasol cake!" exclaimed Flossie. She skipped to a glass case filled with many kinds of fancy pastries. In the middle was a tray of cakes shaped like small, pointed towers. On top of each was a tiny colored paper parasol.

When the treat was served to the Bobbseys at a table, Nan exclaimed, "They're filled with custard!"

After they had eaten the last delicious morsel,

Flossie said, "I even feel sorry for Danny Rugg because he's not in Italy having fun."

"I'll tell you what," said Nan with a twinkle in her eyes. "Let's send him a good surprise instead of a bad one."

They bought a long narrow box of marzipan candies shaped like fruit, which the clerk agreed to send airmail.

"We'll write and tell him we're sending fruit," said Nan, "and when he gets a box of this shape he won't know what to think!"

Freddie laughed. "He'll expect something bad to pop out."

Flossie spied a row of little donkeys made of sugar candy. "Oh, aren't they darling! Let's send one to each of our friends at home."

"Oh yes, let's!" said Nan. "We'll have them all mailed in one box to Nellie's house." Nellie Parks was Nan's best friend.

When they reached the hotel, all but Nan and Flossie went to their rooms on the third floor. The girls stopped in the lobby to write the card to Danny.

"Let's send one to Nellie, too," said Nan.

After mailing the cards, they hurried to the elevator. It was all glass in a dark wood frame.

"This is like Cinderella's coach," said Flossie as the girls stepped inside. Nan pressed the button. Very slowly the cage rose in the well of a spiral staircase made of marble.

Suddenly, as they reached the second floor, both sisters gasped. On the landing stood the bushy-haired man. He was talking to a tall fellow with stringy hair who wore a red-striped shirt.

"Maybe that's Tucci!" Flossie exclaimed.

As she pointed, the man glanced their way. A scowl crossed his narrow face. His close-set eyes looked mean. Quickly he said something to the big man. They hurried down the staircase, as the elevator crept upward.

At the third floor the girls ran out. While Flossie reported to Della, Nan hurried to the boys' room to tell Bert.

"Come on," he exclaimed. "Let's catch them. Maybe they can tell us where Dom is!"

The twins raced down the staircase to the desk in the lobby. "We're looking for a big man with sort of bushy hair," said Bert to the clerk. "Did he—"

"You mean Mr. Gano, from Sicily?" the clerk asked. "He and his friend just went outside."

The twins thanked him and hurried out the front door. At that moment the two men were crossing the street.

"Mr. Gano!" Bert shouted. "Wait! We want to ask you something about Dom Amato."

The men looked back and began to walk quickly. Reaching the far sidewalk, they disappeared down a flight of steps.

The twins hastened across and looked down the

stone steps which led to another street. The men were nowhere in sight.

"Why did they run away?" Nan asked, puzzled.

"It looks suspicious to me," said Bert. He pointed up the street to a small park for the hotel guests. "Let's wait there, and maybe we'll catch Mr. Gano when he comes back."

They walked to the wall which ran across the back of the park and looked out at the twinkling lights of the city and the boats in the harbor. Eight feet below the twins was a narrow sidewalk between the houses and the wall. Bert and Nan seated themselves on a bench and began to talk about Dom's disappearance.

Presently they heard a scraping sound below, and a voice whispered, "Higher. I can't hear."

Bert looked over the wall. Just below was the man in the striped shirt, sitting on Mr. Gano's shoulders!

With a quick movement Bert leaned far over the parapet and grabbed Tucci's shirt.

"Now," the boy exclaimed, "where's Dom Amato?"

Instantly the man leaped off Gano's shoulders. Still holding on, Bert lost his balance and fell over the wall!

CHAPTER V

GIANT JAM

"OW!" yelped Mr. Gano as Bert and the thin man both landed on top of him, knocking him to the ground. Amid grunts, the two men scrambled to their feet and ran down the narrow passage.

"Bert, are you all right?" came Nan's voice.

The boy looked up and saw her leaning over the park wall. "I'm okay," he called and dashed off. "Wait here!"

He followed the men down a stairway to the street on the next level. There he saw them get into a taxi and speed away. Disappointed, the boy slowly climbed the two flights of stairs, met Nan, and together they hurried back to the hotel.

Five minutes later the Bobbseys and Amatos met in Uncle Mario's room and listened to the older twins' story. All were puzzled by the men's strange behavior.

"I think the tall man is Tucci," said Nan.

"And for some reason he's interested in Dom,"

added Mr. Amato. "Probably Gano is, too."

"Maybe they're after the King's Puppet," said Nan. "Remember, the silver armor is valuable."

Bert nodded. "And it's possible they know the secret that Grandfather Martino told his family about. Maybe it's something that makes Orlando worth even more."

"I keep thinking about the eavesdropper at your shop, Uncle Mario," said Nan. "Maybe he came to find out where Dom took the puppet."

"And don't forget Mr. Wood," Flossie spoke up. "He wants Orlando."

"Maybe the two men are working for him," Della remarked.

"I think they're spying on us," said Freddie and told of Gano's question about their hotel. "I guess I let the cat out of the bag," he added sheepishly.

"That's okay," said Nan kindly. "He took you by surprise."

"But you shouldn't be so quick to answer personal questions for strangers," put in Bert.

"I know," Freddie promised. "I won't do it any more."

Della frowned. "What can those men be up to?"

Bert shrugged. "All we know is that it has something to do with Dom and us."

"I think they were eavesdropping to see what our next move will be."

Della yawned. "I think our next move should

be to bed." Later when she and the girls were in their pajamas, Della said, "We'll have breakfast in our rooms tomorrow. That's customary in Italian hotels. I'll eat with Papa, and you and the boys can eat together."

Next morning the girls went to their brothers' room. It was big and sunny. Open double doors led onto a balcony.

"Your room is just like ours," Flossie said. "Let's go outside."

She skipped onto the balcony, and the others crowded after her. They gazed out on the tile-roofed houses which covered the hill below. Beyond lay the blue harbor with a huge gray mountain on the left.

"There's Vesuvius!" said Nan, pointing to the volcano.

Freddie asked, "Does it still blow its top off?"

"It hasn't for a long time," Bert replied. "The worst eruption was in A.D. 79 when it buried the city of Pompeii."

"It was covered with tons of ashes," said Nan, "but now some of it has been dug up, and you can go to see it."

As she spoke, there was a knock at the room door, and Flossie went inside to answer it. A few moments later she called, "Come quick, everybody! A purple fish!"

The others hurried in to see the waiter placing a large tray on a table. Beside a basket of rolls was a pottery pitcher with a purple fish painted on one side.

The waiter smiled. "Fish designs are very popular in Southern Italy," he said. "You see them on cloth, dishes, buildings, and boats—everywhere. That's because fishing is a very important business here."

"I doubt if this is the fish we are looking for," said Bert.

He asked the waiter if he had ever heard of a restaurant or a boat or even a person called the purple fish. The man laughed, shook his head, and left. After breakfast the children met Della in the lobby.

"Papa is going to stay in the hotel in case the police call," she told them. "I've hired a car for us."

She led the twins to the curb where it was parked. Della took the wheel and drove through steep narrow streets down to the waterfront, where she parked near the restaurant.

It was empty except for the singer and the proprietor, who were eating together at a table. On a chair rested the guitar. The owner broke into a stream of Italian when he saw them.

Quickly Della translated. "Dom came back here last night. This man gave him supper and a job washing dishes, then let him sleep in the storeroom behind the kitchen. Dom left an hour ago. The man says he'd have called us, but he lost the piece of paper with our address on it."

"Never mind," said Bert, "does he know where Dom went?"

Della asked, and the proprietor shook his head.

The singer spoke up. "I met him as he was leaving here. I gave him your message."

"What did he say?" chorused the twins.

"He said he would not go back to America. But he did say he would meet you Bobbseys at the hotel tonight."

"Do you know where he is now?" asked Della anxiously.

"He said he was going to take a bus and go to Pompeii to see the ruins."

"Did he have his duffel bag?" Bert asked.

The singer made a face. "Such a heavy thing to carry. He was going to leave it here. I'll ask about it." He spoke to the restaurant owner in Italian. The man replied briefly, then went back to the kitchen.

The singer explained that Dom had wanted to leave the duffel bag in the back room. But when he told the proprietor that the contents were valuable, the man refused to take the responsibility for the bag.

While the Bobbseys had been talking to the man, several people had wandered in and seated themselves at tables.

Nan noticed that a man in a black sleeveless shirt had taken the table behind the singer's. The customer had his back to them, but when he glanced up, Nan saw his face in a mirror on the wall.

"Mr. Tucci!"

Instantly, the man pushed back his chair, grabbed the guitar, and ran for the door. The musician shouted frantically, and the children dashed after Tucci. Swinging the guitar to keep them back, he reached the entrance.

He raised the instrument high in the air, then shouted, "Catch!"

"No, no!" shrieked the musician as Tucci hurled the guitar over the children's heads.

Bert ran backward, leaped and caught it! In the excitement, Tucci disappeared down the street.

"My guitar!" the singer cried and as Bert handed it to him, the man hugged the instrument. "You saved it! I can never thank you enough!" He tried to hug Bert.

"It's all right," said the boy, embarrassed. "Thanks for the help you gave us."

"Come on, let's go," urged Nan. "Tucci heard us say that Dom went to Pompeii. He and Mr. Gano may be after him."

Della agreed. "I don't know what their game is, but I'm afraid they mean harm to Dom."

"Right," said Bert. "We've got to find Dom and that puppet before they do!"

Calling good-by, the searchers hurried out of the restaurant to their car.

As they climbed in, they spotted a small green automobile speeding past.

"There they go!" exclaimed Bert. Tucci was hunched over the wheel with Gano wedged in beside him.

"Hurry, hurry, Della!" Nan said. "What's the quickest way out of town?"

"Through Garibaldi Square," replied Della as she skillfully threaded her way through the heavy traffic.

"Who's Garibaldi?" Flossie asked.

"He was a great Italian hero," Della replied. "Italy used to be lots of little states which kept fighting with each other."

"But Garibaldi helped to make them all into one country," Bert went on. "In 1860 he and his troops unified Sicily and Southern Italy. The first king of the new country was Victor Emmanuel."

"The one who gave Orlando to the Martinos!" exclaimed Freddie.

"That's right," said Della. "Now there's Garibaldi." As they drove into a large busy square, she pointed to a statue on a high pedestal.

"He looks like a very brave man," said Flossie. "What a big beard he had!"

But no one answered her. They all looked worried, for the car was slowing down. Soon they

"Catch!"

had stopped, unable to move in any direction. The huge square was packed tight with automobiles and motorcycles. Horns were honking wildly.

Della groaned. "A giant traffic jam!"

"And we're stuck in it!" exclaimed Freddie.

Nan's heart sank. "If Gano and Tucci got through," she said, "they'll reach Dom before we do!"

CHAPTER VI

TWO SHADOWS

"WILL this traffic jam break up soon?" Flossie asked anxiously.

"I hope so," said Della. "Until it does, we're stuck tight."

Suddenly Freddie cried, "They're moving!" He pointed ahead to where some cars were leaving the square. In a few minutes Della inched forward and finally drove out onto the highway. As they sped past Vesuvius, the children hardly noticed it. They were worried about Dom. What would happen if the two men found him before they did?

In a little while Della turned off the main road. "This is Pompeii," she said, and drove into a parking lot.

While she bought tickets for the ruins, the children looked around trying to spot Dom among the crowds of tourists. But they did not see him.

Quickly Della led the Bobbseys to the brick

51

walls of the ancient city. They walked under an arch and up a steep passage paved with smooth stones.

"This is one of the seven gates to Pompeii," she explained.

At the top they came out into a bright sunlit street.

"Wait!" Nan said. "I have an idea. That duffel bag is so heavy, I don't think Dom will carry it around with him. I bet he'll hide it somewhere, and pick it up later."

"I get it," said Freddie. "If we see the bag, all we have to do is wait there and catch him when he comes for it."

"If Gano and Tucci don't find him first," Bert murmured.

"Another thing," said Della, "it's very crowded. If we get separated, let's meet in half an hour at the refreshment center."

"Maybe we should look for Dom there first," said Freddie hopefully. "It's so hot, I bet he'll want a soda."

But the others ignored the hint and started walking along the narrow streets with high curbs. Della pointed out the ruts made by chariot wheels in the lava paving stones.

"Those grooves are over a thousand years old," she said.

Now and then they stopped to look into low brick buildings which had once been shops.

"You can see the counters in the front," Nan remarked.

"And bowls and vats where the food was kept," Bert added.

"When the city was excavated," Della said, "things were found just as they had been the day the volcano erupted. Pots, pans, dishes—everything was just where the fleeing people left it."

The sun was blazing hot, and soon the smaller twins lagged behind. Suddenly Freddie pointed through a low iron gate at some ruins almost overgrown by high grass. "Look! I see something red!"

The children slipped through the gate and hurried toward the spot. There in the weeds lay a duffel bag! A bit of red plume was sticking out the top.

Quickly Flossie peeked into the bag. "It's Orlando!"

"Maybe Dom's in these ruins," Freddie said.

The children looked around at the crumbling buildings. In the distance against the bright blue sky loomed the gray cone of Mt. Vesuvius. Nothing moved. All was silent.

"Let's look in the houses, Freddie," Flossie suggested. They walked toward the nearest one and peered in the open doorway.

"It's dark in there," Freddie said.

"Dom?" Flossie called. No answer.

Cautiously the children stepped inside. After

the bright sunlight, they could see nothing. But in a few minutes, they made out a bare room with a tile floor.

Freddie drew in his breath. "Ooh, look at the picture!"

Painted onto the wall were green trees, flowers, and brick-red birds with long necks.

"People in Pompeii must have loved pretty gardens," said Flossie, "if they even wanted them inside their houses."

The twins walked to the window and looked out toward the duffel bag.

Suddenly Flossie seized her brother's hand and pointed to the wall of the next house. There was the huge shadow of a man with a large hat.

"Oh-oh!" whispered Freddie. "I'll bet it's the bad man!"

As he spoke, the shadow moved and a tall thin one appeared beside it.

Quickly the children ducked below the window ledge, then cautiously peeked over it.

"Oh," whispered Flossie, "they've seen the duffel bag!"

Tucci's long legs swished through the grass, and he squatted down beside the puppet. He fingered the red plume and grinned up at Gano.

The two men talked quickly together. But neither one picked up the bag.

"I bet they're going to wait here for Dom,"

"I'll bet it's the bad man!" whispered Freddie

said Freddie softly. "We've got to warn him. Maybe we—" He stopped short.

There was Dom, striding toward the duffel bag!

"Dom!" cried the twins. "Look out!"

As the boy glanced around in surprise, Tucci bounded to the bag and swung it to his shoulder.

Dom whirled. "Hey, that's mine! Put it down!" he shouted.

Tucci pushed him aside and strode toward the gate. At the same time Gano ran over and grabbed the boy's arm.

"You're coming with us," he ordered sharply, "—down to the purple fish!"

Dom broke loose and dashed after Tucci.

"No, no! Don't go!" the twins cried.

As they raced out the doorway to help Dom, they ran right into Gano.

"Mind your own business!" he growled and gave them a hard push. They stumbled backward against each other and fell into the house. Unhurt, they scrambled up and ran out.

The big man was shoving Dom through the gate. "Bring back my bag!" the boy yelled to Tucci.

"Stop!" the children shouted racing after them. Suddenly a large party of tourists came out of a side street, blocking the road.

"Excuse us," said Flossie and the twins plunged into the crowd. When they came out, Dom and his captors were gone.

"We've got to find Bert and the others," said Freddie, panting.

By asking people, the children found the refreshment center. The older twins and Della were at a table sipping cool drinks.

Hot and breathless, Freddie and Flossie reported what had happened.

Bert's eyes snapped with excitement. "You're sure Gano said, '*down* to the purple fish'? That might mean they're heading south."

Della agreed. "They're probably going down the Amalfi Coast," she said. "There are lots of little fishing villages where they may try to hide Dom."

While she paid the bill, Bert and Nan put clean straws in their drinks and told their thirsty brother and sister to finish them.

Not long afterward the searchers were on a narrow road winding along a cliff. Over a low stone wall on their right, they could see the blue sea far below.

"It can't be Orlando the men are after," Bert remarked, "or they wouldn't have bothered with Dom."

Nan spoke up. "One thing's sure, they can't all squeeze in that little car with the puppet." She guessed that one of the men would have to join the others later.

At each town and village on the way Della asked people if they had seen the green car. At first the answers were all no. Then she questioned a boy mounting a motorcycle at the side of the road.

He replied rapidly, then zoomed away.

Della called, "*Grazie!* Thank you!" and drove on. "We're on the right track," she said. "He noticed the duffel bag and described the driver. It's Tucci."

Later she found several other people who had spotted the boy and his captor. The trail led on down the coast.

Suddenly Nan cried, "Look! Their car!" She had spied a small green automobile parked on a terrace just below the road wall.

Della slowed down and backed up.

"It looks like the one," Bert agreed, "but we can't be sure. Too bad we don't know their license number."

Below the empty car, the hillside was a jumble of huge boulders and wide ledges which ended at a sandy beach. Near the bottom they could see a handful of houses.

"That's one of the smallest fishing villages on this coast," Della told them.

"The men could be holding Dom there," said Nan. "Let's go down and take a look around."

"Okay," said Della. She backed up a little farther, steered down a rough drive to the terrace and parked near the little car.

They got out and made their way along a steep

narrow path between high rocks. Finally they came out among the houses which straggled down toward the beach. There half a dozen fishing boats were pulled up on the sand.

"Where is everyone?" Flossie asked, puzzled. No one was in sight.

"It's almost one o'clock," said Della, glancing at her watch. "They're probably taking siestas."

"Hello!" Bert called. "Anybody here?"

No answer.

Bert looked around at the small stucco houses with their dark windows. Beaded curtains hung in the doorways, and one of them moved slightly.

"Someone's watching," Bert thought.

"Maybe we'd better eat lunch and come back later," Della suggested.

The twins agreed and they started up the path. Nan was last, and as the others disappeared around a big rock, she stopped. Somewhere a woman was singing softly! The voice seemed to be coming from a house on a rocky ledge away from the others. Quietly Nan climbed up to it. She paused outside the beaded curtain.

"Hello!" she called softly.

The singing stopped.

Nan was about to call again when she glanced at the wall beside the door. Her heart gave a thump!

There was the faded drawing of a purple fish!

CHAPTER VII

THE PURPLE FISH

NAN stared at the telltale sign on the wall of
the house. "If Dom's a prisoner in there," she
thought, "Tucci may be with him. I'd better run
for help."

Just then the beaded curtain in the doorway
swished aside. A young woman stood there, holding a baby. She had long dark hair and her big
eyes were frightened. She seized Nan's wrist and
drew her into the house.

In the gloom Nan could make out several tables
with chairs and a counter at one side. The place
was a tiny coffee shop. No one else was there.

"Dom Amato," Nan said softly, "is he—"

Quickly the woman put her finger to her lips.
"Go red-eye," she whispered brokenly. "No help
here—all afraid of Tucci."

Suddenly a heavy step sounded in the next
room. Swiftly the woman pushed Nan out the
door. "Red-eye," she repeated. "Run!"

Nan scrambled down the rocks, then climbed the path to the terrace without stopping. At the top the others were waiting.

"What kept you?" asked Bert.

"I've found Dom!" Nan gasped. Quickly she told all about the woman in the *Purple Fish*. "I bet he's a prisoner there."

"We need the police," Della decided quickly. "Come on!"

"Why don't we rescue Dom ourselves?" protested Freddie, as they all piled into the car.

"Too risky," said Della. "Tucci's dangerous!" She gunned the motor, zoomed backward up the drive onto the road, then drove swiftly ahead.

"We'll get help in the town of Amalfi," she said. "It's not far from here."

"It's a famous place, isn't it?" asked Nan.

"Sure," said Bert. "The whole shore is known as the Amalfi Coast, and this road we are on is called the Amalfi Drive."

"The coast is well known because it's so beautiful," said Della. "Lots of people come for vacations. There's the hotel!" she added.

Ahead was a large white stucco building with pink flowers growing up one wall. Della went up the curving drive and parked at the side.

"I'll call the police," Della said as they got out of the car. "You order a quick lunch for us all. Don't wait for me. Start eating!"

She dashed toward the door. The children hurried inside after her and found their way to a large dining porch.

They seated themselves at a table and ordered *lasagna* and salad.

Then Freddie hopped up and gazed over the porch railing at the colored umbrellas on the beach below. Beyond sparkled the bright blue water of the Tyrrhenian Sea. Suddenly he squinted hard at a yellow fishing boat which was heading out to sea.

"Look!" Freddie cried. "A red eye!"

As the children ran over he pointed to the boat. The prow was decorated to look like a fish-head. Painted on it was a huge red eye!

"Oh, that's what the woman meant!" exclaimed Nan in dismay. "Dom must be on that boat."

Bert shaded his eyes. "There's a man with a black shirt at the wheel. It looks like Tucci."

"I don't see Dom or Orlando," said Freddie.

"They're probably down in the cabin," Bert replied.

Flossie plucked the sleeve of a passing waiter. "Please, where is that boat going?" she asked.

The man smiled and shrugged. "Maybe Sicily," he replied. "It's the right direction."

"I'll bet that is where it's bound," said Nan. "The hotel clerk told us Gano is from there."

Bert nodded. "He may be with them by now or on his way to get a plane to Sicily."

"Look! A red eye!"

Just then Della returned and the twins poured out the news and pointed to the craft, which was fast disappearing.

"Oh, no!" Della cried, ruffling her short hair. "Now what'll we do?"

"Inform the Naples police and have them contact the authorities in Sicily," said Bert. "Maybe they can catch the *Red Eye* when it lands."

"Right," said Della and hurried off to call again. When she returned lunch was on the table and the twins were eating hungrily. As Della helped herself, she told them that everything had been taken care of with the Amalfi and Naples police. "I called Papa, too, and he is arranging for us to go to Sicily tonight."

"By plane?" Bert asked.

"I don't know. We'll have to hurry back and find out!"

But as they were leaving the hotel, the manager called to Della. "*Signorina Amato? Telefono.*"

Della followed the man to the telephone, and the children went to the car to wait for her. A few minutes later she swung into the driver's seat. "That was Papa. There are no flights available. We're to go straight to the Palermo steamer."

Flossie bounced in excitement. "Oh goody! A boat! How long does it take to get there?"

"Overnight," Della replied as she headed the car for Naples.

Each time they approached a curve in the narrow Amalfi Drive, Della honked the horn long and hard. On the way down, she had explained that this was the customary way to let approaching drivers know your car was coming.

The traffic had been light then, but now, time after time, there came answering honks from around the curve. Slowly the Bobbseys' car would inch around while the other waited, crowded against the rocky cliff.

"It's a close shave," Bert remarked.

"I hope we don't miss the boat," Flossie thought anxiously.

It was after six o'clock when they reached the dock and saw Uncle Mario surrounded by all their baggage.

He rushed to the car. "I thought you'd never come!" he exclaimed. Mopping his brow, he told them everything was arranged. "Della, you can turn in the car here. I sent for a man from the rental office to pick it up."

As the children piled out, he signaled an attendant, who came over and took the wheel.

"We sail at eight," said Uncle Mario, "but we'll go on board now for dinner."

A porter took their bags up the gangplank, and a steward showed them to two staterooms. Each had three single bunks in it.

Flossie giggled as she saw the metal railing around each one. "Is that so we don't fall out?"

Nan laughed. "If the ship rolls in a storm, you'll be glad to have a fence."

When the girls had washed and dressed they strolled along the deck to the dining room where they met Mr. Amato and the boys. Over a delicious fish dinner, the Bobbseys told Uncle Mario all that had happened that day. By the time they finished, it was dark and through the windows they could see the lights of other ships in the harbor.

"Dom kidnapped!" said Mr. Amato and shook his head. "I can't believe it."

"Don't worry," said Bert firmly. "We're going to find him and solve the mystery."

"You're very clever children," said Mr. Amato, "but if Tucci manages to land with Dom in Sicily and get by the police, your job will be very hard."

"Why?" asked Nan.

"Because there are so many places to hide on the island—mountains, seacoasts, crowded cities, lonely countrysides! Why, bandits have been known to stay in the hills for years without being caught."

The little man gave a huge sigh and gazed gloomily at his empty plate.

"Come on, Uncle Mario," said Freddie. "You must be brave, like Garibaldi."

Suddenly there was a rumbling beneath them.

"The engines!" exclaimed Freddie. "We're going!"

The children asked to be excused and hurried to the rail to watch the sailors cast off. Afterward the twins explored the ship.

Then Flossie said, "Let's go and watch TV in the coffee lounge."

Nan and Freddie went with her, but Bert walked to the bow and stood by the rail in the darkness. The deck was deserted. He listened to the rush of the water beneath him and felt the wind whip his hair. The dark shapes of large islands slid by. His thoughts went to the little boat *Red Eye* far ahead of him at sea.

"It'll get to Sicily before we do," he worried, "and then—"

Suddenly he heard a soft step behind him. A huge hand was clapped over his mouth and he was swooped up above the rail.

"I ought to throw you in the sea!" came a hoarse whisper.

CHAPTER VIII

A BLUE TOY

"THIS is a warning," Bert's attacker went on, his hand tightening over the boy's mouth. "Forget Dom Amato!"

For another moment the man held Bert over the ship's rail. Then he set him down roughly, yanked a cloth bag over his head and tied it on.

When Bert finally freed himself the deck was empty.

"That was Gano, I bet," he thought and hurried to the coffee lounge, where he found the other twins with Della and Mr. Amato.

Quickly Bert told what had happened. Della grew pale. Her father jumped up and exclaimed, "We will report it to the captain! Gano can't get away with this!"

"But, I can't prove it was Gano," Bert reminded him. "So far as I know, there was no one around and I didn't even see his face." Bert was still carrying the bag.

"A pillowcase," said Della, taking it from him. "I'll give it back to the steward."

Mr. Amato led the children to the purser, who took them to see the captain in his cabin. A thin, stern man, he listened to Bert's story and then to Freddie and Flossie's account of the kidnapping in Pompeii.

"I will radio the Palermo police," he said. "They can pick up this man when we dock."

"Maybe it would be better to shadow him," Bert suggested, "if Dom has not been found."

"That's right," the captain said. "Gano might lead them to the boy."

That night the travelers went to bed hoping they would see Dom next day. Flossie dreamed that Mr. Gano was a giant rocking the big boat. She woke up clinging to her bed rail.

It was morning. Della and Nan were already dressed. "Come on, sleepyhead," Nan said, smiling. "We're almost to Sicily."

In a short time Flossie was ready, wearing a straw hat and carrying a pocketbook to match.

A little while after breakfast, the boat docked and the passengers began to swarm off. Someone pushed past the Bobbseys roughly. It was Gano! He was wearing dark glasses. Tipping his black hat, he gave a wolfish grin.

"I'd like to punch him in the nose," muttered Mr. Amato.

"Now Papa," said Della, "leave him to the police."

The Bobbseys followed the Amatos to a small bus with the name of their hotel on the side. Uncle Mario asked the driver to take the luggage to the hotel, but to let them off near Aunt Bartolina's house. "We must see her right away," he told the others.

As the bus drove away, Bert noticed Gano standing near a taxi, watching them go. "Now he knows where we are staying," the boy thought, and hoped the police had spotted the man.

Soon the bus turned down a wide avenue and stopped at a side street.

As the Bobbsey party got out, about a dozen children came running up to meet them. Uncle Mario spoke to them and several ran shouting to a house a few doors away.

A moment later, a stout woman wearing a black dress and flowered apron burst out the door. Her dark hair was pulled back tight into a bun and her round face beamed.

"Mario! Della!" she cried, embracing and kissing them.

Mr. Amato introduced the twins, and Aunt Bartolina kissed and hugged them, too.

Then the woman said, "Dom? Mio Dom?"

"Please," said Mr. Amato, "let's go inside."

He pushed Aunt Bartolina gently through the beaded curtains into her front room. Several straight chairs stood around a center table with a red cloth on it. The linoleum floor was shining clean.

The stout woman seized Uncle Mario by the lapels, and began to talk swiftly in her own tongue.

As Mr. Amato replied, she flung both arms into the air and gave a loud cry. She collapsed, sobbing, on a chair.

While she cried, her relatives and the Bobbseys tried to comfort her in Italian and English.

At last she looked up with streaming eyes. Flossie took a little white handkerchief from her pocketbook and offered it to her.

"Ah!" the woman cried and gave Flossie a squeeze which set her straw hat on edge. "*Grazie!*"

But she tucked the handkerchief back into the little girl's hand and half-laughing, wiped her eyes on her apron.

Mr. Amato stood up. "This very minute I am going to the police. Perhaps they have news already!"

As he turned to go, a child's head poked through the door curtains. She was about seven and had straight black hair which hung down to her eyebrows. She stared curiously at the children.

"Bibi!" said Aunt Bartolina and beckoned.

The child vanished.

The big woman sighed. "Bibi Martino." She shook her head disapprovingly.

When Mr. Amato had gone, Dom's mother spoke quickly to Della, who translated. "Come, we will go see the Martinos."

Aunt Bartolina led the way across the street to a house with large puppets painted on the peeling plaster wall. They went past a tiny ticket counter and through shabby red curtains into a little theater filled with benches. On the lighted stage was a husky, gray-haired man adjusting the rods on a puppet.

Aunt Bartolina called to him and he came down to greet the visitors, as the other puppeteers came hurrying from backstage.

The stout woman introduced the children, then pointed to the gray-haired man. "Papa Martino."

"And this is Mama," he said with a flourish toward his wife. She was a big dark-haired woman, taller than he was. She flashed a smile and pointed to three handsome young men in dark trousers. Below their rolled-up sleeves bulged huge muscles.

"My sons—Emilio, Stefano, Vince. They work the *marionetti*," she added proudly. "Papa talks all the parts."

"And Mama plays the piano," said her husband.

The woman pulled forward a fourth boy, about eighteen years old. He was slender and had dark hair which curled almost to his ears. "This is

Peppo." She patted his shoulder. "A good boy, my Peppo, but he is not strong enough to handle the puppets."

"He helps polish armor, though," said Vince.

"His real job is running a motorboat,'" put in Stefano. "He takes out tourists."

Peppo grinned. "Where's Bibi?"

All together the Martinos shouted, "BIBI!" But the child did not come.

"Gone again!" exclaimed Mama Martino. "Bibi is my niece from the country," she explained. "Her mother and father died two years ago, and since then she has lived with us. But I cannot keep track of her. Where is Dom?" she added. "Bartolina said he was coming."

The twins and Della then told what had happened to Dom.

The Martinos' eyes were round as saucers. "He found Orlando!" cried Papa. "The King's Puppet!"

Anxiously the puppeteers talked about the missing boy. Questions and answers flew quickly.

Finally Nan said, "It's wonderful how you all speak English."

Emilio stroked his thin mustache. "We learned in order to give special performances for tourists."

"But business is terrible," said Papa sadly. "I don't know how much longer our theater will last."

All the Martinos looked gloomy. Then Vince smiled at the younger twins. "You are just the size of our puppets," he said.

"Look at me, Freddie," said Peppo. "This is how the puppets walk!" He stuck out his chest and swinging his legs stiffly, stalked along, swaying from side to side.

Freddie laughed and tried it himself. "Very good," exclaimed Vince. "Every Sicilian schoolboy knows that trick."

"Everybody come next door," Mama Martino commanded. "We will have lunch. There is plenty!"

The visitors followed the Martinos through a small door at the side of the stage and up a few stairs. As they passed through the dimly lit backstage area, Freddie noticed a suit of puppet armor and a helmet on a table. At one end of the wing they went through a door into a big sunny kitchen.

"Umm, something smells yummy!" thought Flossie.

While Mama Martino served from a huge pot on the stove, Nan looked out a door into the back yard. She heard a cat meowing, but could not see one. "It's around the corner, I guess," she thought.

Soon everyone was seated at the big round table including Bibi, though Nan had not seen her come in.

Heaping plates of ravioli with rich tomato sauce

were passed. Mama Martino handed Bert a jar.

"Grated cheese," she said. "You sprinkle on top."

"Grazie," said Bert and took off the lid. For a moment he could not believe what he saw.

"A blue mouse!" he exclaimed, pulling out a little catnip toy.

Peppo was laughing and Bibi was grinning.

"How did a toy mouse get in the jar?" asked Flossie, wide-eyed.

"The mystery cat," said Mama Martino, shaking her head while Aunt Bartolina clucked disapprovingly. "Somebody has been playing tricks in this neighborhood—everyday something happens. Last week Grandma Ferrara's black stockings were hanging over the balcony. They disappeared and she found a link of sausages there instead. That same day I missed a garlic from my kitchen and found an orange in its place."

"And each time," said Vince, "when the trick is discovered, a cat is heard meowing."

Peppo recovered his breath. "The meow is the joker's signature."

"This must be the mystery Aunt Bartolina wrote Dom about," thought Nan.

When lunch was over, the men and boys sat at the table and talked, while the girls helped Mama Martino clean up the kitchen.

When the last dish had been dried, Flossie remembered that she had left her pocketbook on a

"A blue mouse!"

bench in the theater. She went through the door into the backstage area. It was dark and she felt her way down the steps into the theater.

Suddenly she heard a soft clanking. She smiled. "I won't get fooled again."

She ran her hand along the benches until she grasped her purse. At that moment a blue light flooded the stage!

Flossie's eyes grew wide with fright. Out clanked an armored knight with the helmet visor down. But no rods were connected to the figure!

"Help! Nan!" she screeched. "It's a puppet come to life!"

CHAPTER IX

THE PAINTED CART

THE puppet stopped short. Stiffly it faced the front of the stage. Then suddenly it began to giggle!

"Freddie Bobbsey!" exclaimed Flossie, as the boy lifted the visor of his helmet.

Just then Nan came down the steps into the theater, as Bert and Peppo appeared on the stage.

"What's going on here?" Nan asked.

"I scared Flossie!" exclaimed Freddie. He flapped his elbows. "How'm I going to get out of this armor? It's hard to move."

"Maybe we ought to leave you in it," said Bert, with a wink at Peppo.

The older boy was grinning. "We'd better get him out," he said. "Papa needs the armor."

While he and Bert helped the little boy take off the costume, Nan and Flossie went backstage to look around. On a shelf were several helmeted heads in a row and lying on a table below them, two headless puppet bodies.

Carrying the armor, Peppo came over. "Sometimes one knight has to play several parts," he explained, "so we just stick a different head on him."

Freddie touched one of the bodies. "This armor looks like silver," he said.

"It's brass and nickel-plated," Peppo told him.

"But the other suit looks like gold," Flossie remarked.

Peppo smiled. "That's supposed to," he said, "but it's plain brass. A certain few characters always wear the gold-colored armor."

Bert pointed to a platform which crossed above the stage. "Is that where the men stand to work the puppets?" Peppo nodded.

Freddie pointed to a small switchboard. "That's where I turned on the stage light," he said proudly. "I was just trying on the armor when I heard Flossie come, so I decided to scare her."

His twin giggled.

Peppo tossed the armor on the table. "That suit's awfully battered. All the costumes are shabby," he added sadly, "and the scenery is, too."

"Can't you get new things?" Flossie asked.

"We haven't enough money," Peppo replied. "People don't come to see our show the way they used to, because everything looks so old."

He led them to a row of puppets hanging on a rack. "Look at the poor things," he said. The children saw that some knights had no armor, but wore faded doublets. Several lady puppets hung beside them in worn velvet gowns.

Flossie shook her head sadly. "I think they would like new dresses."

"Cheer up, Peppo," Nan said. "Maybe we'll find Dom soon and then you'll have the King's Puppet back. Lots of people will come to see him, I bet."

"I'll show you where we used to keep him," said Peppo. He led them out to a corner of the auditorium where an empty glass case rested on a pedestal. "Here's where he stood on exhibition. He was magnificent! Mama kept his armor so bright and shining! And everybody knew the story of the King's Puppet," he added. "They always stopped to admire him.

"But a couple of years ago robbers broke in, smashed the glass, and took Orlando." Peppo explained that his father had installed a new case, hoping the puppet would be recovered.

"Do you think the robbers knew the secret about Orlando?" Bert asked.

"No. Only Grandfather Martino did." Suddenly Peppo's eyes sparkled. "Grandfather was a great old man—a real showman. His hair was long and white and he always wore a cape and carried a cane. How he loved to pull dramatic surprises! Besides, he always had candy and little presents in his pockets for my brothers and me."

"He sounds like fun," said Bert.

"Oh, he was," said Peppo. "Then one day ten years ago he announced he was taking a vacation trip to Milan. The family didn't want him to go because he was very old and hadn't been feeling well, but he went anyway. He came back a week later and told us that there was a secret about Orlando and we would all find out in three days."

"And then what?" asked Freddie eagerly.

Peppo looked sad. "Two days later he died suddenly. The trip had been too much for him." The boy went on to say that the family had decided that the grandfather must have learned something important about the puppet in Milan. "We studied the history of the king and Garibaldi thinking the secret might have to do with them, but discovered no clue."

"Did you examine Orlando?" Bert asked.

"Yes, but we found nothing."

"How about the case and the pedestal?" Nan asked.

"Stefano took them apart. He saw nothing unusual." Peppo went on, "There was one other odd thing. Grandfather had taken most of his savings to Milan with him, and all of that money was gone."

"Maybe he was robbed," said Bert.

"What a strange mystery," said Nan. "And

only the King's Puppet knows the answer."

Peppo led the way back to the stage and turned out the blue light. Then the children followed him through the kitchen into the Martinos' front room.

Now Uncle Mario was there with the others. Everyone looked worried. The police had not located the *Red Eye.*

"None of the seacoast towns have reported it," said Mr. Amato. "Maybe it didn't come to Sicily."

"What about Gano?" asked Nan.

"The officers followed him to a restaurant," said Uncle Mario. "After a while, several people came out, but not Gano. Finally the police went in, but he was gone. Vanished!"

As the elder Martinos shook their heads, Peppo suggested that the Bobbseys take a sightseeing tour around Palermo. "I'll be your guide," he offered.

Mr. Amato agreed at once. "It's time they had some fun."

After thanking Mama Martino for the lunch, the three Amatos and the children walked with Peppo to the hotel on a nearby boulevard. The desk clerk ordered a car for them and gave Bert a small map of the city.

With Peppo driving, the Bobbseys set off through downtown Palermo. They passed a magnificent, domed opera house, an ancient Norman arch, and many restaurants with sidewalk tables. Nowhere did they see Gano.

Then Peppo said they would go to a museum in a big park. On the way they stopped at a pottery store to do some shopping.

They were greeted by a thin little woman with curly black hair. In careful English she told them that her name was Signora Donna and that she owned the shop. "Making pottery is an important business in Sicily," she added.

The Bobbseys bought a big jar with a funny face on it for their parents and had it shipped home. For themselves the children picked out small brightly colored plaques shaped like fish.

After Nan paid, the younger twins peeked into a large whitewashed room behind the shop.

"What's that big round thing with the door in front?" Flossie asked Signora Donna.

"The kiln, where I bake the pottery."

But Freddie was eyeing a large black hat resting on a table beside the oven.

"Whose is that?" he asked the woman.

She frowned. "Someone left it here," she said nervously and placed her arm across the doorway. "Don't go in there, please."

As soon as the children were outside, Freddie exclaimed, "I bet it was Gano's hat."

Nan laughed. "Now, Freddie, Gano doesn't have the only black hat in Palermo."

When they reached the museum, Peppo led them to a room in which there were several large two-wheeled carts. On the sides of them were colorful paintings of knights in battle.

"What bee-yoo-tiful pictures!" exclaimed Flossie. "That one knight looks like Orlando!"

"*Si*," said a soft voice. The children turned to face a thin young man wearing horn-rimmed glasses. He told them he was Dr. Panito, a curator of the museum, and the children introduced themselves.

"Sicilian carts often had pictures of Charlemagne's knights on them," he said. "The peasants used to build and decorate the carts, but no more. Those we have are precious now. Here's another treasure," Dr. Panito went on, and showed them a glass case of coins.

"They look really ancient," remarked Bert.

"These are Greek, Roman, and Arabian," he replied. "Sicily has had many invaders, and the coins they left behind are collectors' items. Last year an old man wanted to give his coin collection to this museum, but we never got it."

"What happened?" Bert asked.

"A scoundrel named Vito bullied the poor old fellow into giving it to him."

"Vito!" the children chorused.

"We know a Carlo Vito," said Nan, "a big bald man. He's been trying to force Mr. Amato into selling him an ice cream recipe."

"Don't go in there, please!"

"He sounds like the same one," said Dr. Panito, and his eyes snapped angrily. "That's Vito's game—he threatens people into doing what he wants. He makes them afraid to go to the police. So far it's been impossible to get evidence on him. He's a slippery fish!"

"He's not the only slippery one," said Bert, and told the curator about their search for Dom and the King's Puppet.

Dr. Panito exclaimed in admiration. "What brave children you are! I would like to do something for you. Come."

He led them to an inner room where he opened a large closet filled with clothes.

"These are Sicilian national costumes," he said. Quickly he sorted out four small sizes.

"Put them on over your clothes," he said with a smile. "Then come with me."

"Oh, they're so bright and gay!" exclaimed Nan.

She and Flossie slipped on long, full red skirts with bright blue aprons. On top they wore white blouses with black bodices. Meanwhile Bert and Freddie put on dark green coats, knee pants, scarlet sashes, and black boots.

Dr. Panito led them to a winding driveway. There stood a Sicilian cart with a small donkey harnessed to it. The little animal wore red plumes on his head and in the middle of his back.

The curator took a camera from his pocket. "I

was about to take a picture of this. Now you will be in the cart!"

While Peppo watched, the children climbed in and Bert took the reins.

Suddenly a small car zoomed around the curve, straight for the cart!

"Watch out!" Bert shouted as the children screamed. The donkey bolted, tipping the cart. All spilled out!

The little car swerved and sped out of the grounds.

As Peppo caught the donkey and righted the cart, Dr. Panito helped the children up.

"Are you hurt?" he asked anxiously, and the children said they were not.

"That man—it was Tucci!" Bert exclaimed.

"Where Tucci is, Dom must be!" exclaimed Nan. "We must tell Uncle Mario right away!"

"Wait," cried Dr. Panito. "One picture—please! I will send it to your parents!"

Swiftly the children mounted the cart, and the photograph was taken. They they ran back to the museum and carefully removed the costumes. After thanking Dr. Panito, they headed for the hotel.

"Listen," said Peppo excitedly, "the man I work for has a motorboat. Maybe he'll let us take it this evening and search for the *Red Eye*."

"That's a great idea!" said Bert. "Call him from the hotel."

Peppo made the call, then came out of the booth grinning. "It's okay! We can go!"

Right after supper the motorboat roared across the blue water with Peppo at the wheel. Bert was beside him and Nan in the back seat with her arm around Bibi.

"Where are Freddie and Flossie?" the little girl asked.

"They went for a ride with Della," Nan replied.

Peppo cruised slowly along the coast of the island. At dusk their boat rounded a huge promontory. Peppo pointed out dark openings at the base of the brown and green cliffs. "Grottoes," he shouted. "Too small for the *Red Eye*."

"We've heard of the Blue Grotto," said Nan, "the one on the island of Capri."

"That's near Naples," said Peppo. "You passed it last night on the boat. There are lots of blue grottoes in this part of the world," he went on, "but that one is the most famous."

"What makes the water in them so blue?" asked Bert.

"I don't know exactly. It has something to do with the way the light comes through the opening of the grotto," replied the boy. "There are emerald grottoes, too, where the water is green."

Peppo cruised farther up the shore where they found coves and inlets to examine. When it was dark, they gave up and sped toward Palermo.

Suddenly Bert spotted a small yellow light wavering at the base of the promontory. Then the boat was past and the flare was out of sight. "Go back!" he cried. "I think I saw a torch!"

"But that's a straight rock wall," Peppo said. "There is no place for anyone to stand and hold a torch."

"It was very close to the water," said Bert.

"Maybe the torch was in a grotto," Nan suggested.

Peppo swung the craft around in a big circle and cruised back toward the place where Bert had cried out.

There was no light!

CHAPTER X

THE MYSTERY CAT

"ARE you sure you saw a light, Bert?" Nan asked.

"I think so," he replied, peering across the dark water.

"I'm afraid to run the boat any closer to the cliff," said Peppo. "The sea's getting rough."

Nan glanced up and saw that the sky was starless. The wind was rising.

"A storm's coming up," said Bibi.

"We can't hang around here long," Peppo added.

For a few minutes he ran the craft back along the way they had come. Bert turned on the boat's searchlight and aimed it at the cliffs. They could see the low, black mouths of the grottoes, but there was no boat or any sign of life.

"Sometimes men fish in the grottoes at night," said Peppo. "You probably saw one of their torches."

He swung the boat around and sped homeward once again. But by the time they docked, the clouds had blown away and the moon was out.

Nan suggested that they get ice cream. "Bert and I'll treat," she said.

Bibi grasped Nan's hand and skipped happily along as Peppo led them to the tree-lined boulevard which lay along the waterfront. Along the wide sidewalk were small grassy parks and beyond them were old buildings with broken decorations.

"Some of those were palaces once," said Peppo. "But now they're apartment houses."

In front of one of the palaces were chairs and tables under a string of white light bulbs.

The children seated themselves and Bibi said, "I'll take what Peppo takes."

Her cousin grinned. "And she goes wherever I go, too," he said.

The children ordered Sicilian ice cream. When it came, Nan took a spoonful, then said, "This is good, but you should taste Uncle Mario's."

As she and Bert described the Amato ice cream, Peppo listened eagerly. His own ice cream melted in the dish and his eyes were bright. "Wouldn't I like to see him make it!" he exclaimed.

"So would I," said Bibi. "We could go to New York!"

"A trip to America costs money," said Peppo.

"I'll earn it," declared Bibi. "I'm going to sell my jar."

Peppo laughed. "You and your jar! When are you going to let me see it?"

"Maybe never," said Bibi with a grin. "When I gave you a chance, you wouldn't look."

"I was busy."

"Where did you get it?" Nan asked.

"I found it in a field."

"In Agrigento," Peppo explained. "That's where she used to live. In ancient times it was a Greek town. You can see ruins of temples there."

"What does your jar look like?" Nan asked.

"Oh, it's just an old jar," said Bibi. "But somebody might need one and buy it," she added hopefully. "It only has one little crack in it."

"Have you tried to sell it?" Nan asked.

"Yes," said Bibi. "I keep asking people, but everybody's too busy to look at it. Like that man this morning," she added. "He was peeking in the theater when you were there, but he walked away and wouldn't talk to me."

When they had finished the ice cream, Peppo and Bibi thanked the Bobbseys and the children parted.

At the hotel, Bert and Nan found the young twins in the lobby with the Amatos.

"We drove up on a mounain," said Flossie, "and looked straight across the Mediterranean Sea. We could almost see Africa."

Bert smiled. "No you couldn't, Floss. Africa's too far away."

After he and Nan had reported on the boat trip, the travelers went to bed. As Flossie was drifting off to sleep, she heard a lion roar. "I was right," she thought. "Africa is closer than Bert thinks."

At breakfast she told the others about it.

"The lion wasn't in Africa," said Nan. "Maybe there's a lion around the hotel," she suggested, laughing.

"In downtown Palermo?" said Freddie. "Ha-ha-ha."

Bert grinned. "I'll tell you what. We'll take a walk and if we meet a lion, I'll buy you girls a soda."

Della's eyes twinkled. "There's a park on the next corner. Why don't you start there?"

Carrying their pottery fish, the young twins followed the older ones through a high iron gate into the park, then walked down a tree-shaded path. It led to a small zoo. And there was a lion!

"I was wrong!" said Bert laughing.

"So was I," said Flossie, "about Africa."

Bert led the way to a vendor under a striped umbrella and bought sodas for everyone. When they had all finished, the older twins went off to explore the park.

Freddie and Flossie sat on the grass near a big clump of bushes and began to play fish market. Flossie put out her fat blue pottery fish and Freddie placed his lavender octopus next to it.

Suddenly they heard a loud meow!

"Let's see if that's a real cat," Flossie whispered. She and her brother tiptoed toward a clump of trees from which the noise had come. They walked in and looked all around, but saw no one.

As they came out, Flossie cried, "The mystery cat!" A thin arm in a black cotton stocking was coming out of the bushes with a red ball in the hand. It placed the toy on the grass.

"My octopus!" Freddie cried. "It's gone!"

As the twins raced toward the black arm, it vanished and they heard scrambling in the bushes. They plunged into the shrubbery and thrashed about, but found no one. Bursting out again, they met Nan and Bert.

"What's the matter?" asked Nan. "You're full of leaves!" The young twins poured out their story.

"The mystery cat may still be in the park," said Nan.

"Listen," said Freddie excitedly, "the arm was very thin, so I think it's a child. If we go up to all the children we see and say 'meow,' the one who is the cat will look guilty. Watch me."

Freddie darted up to two thin girls who were throwing bread into the bear cage. "MEOW," said Freddie loudly.

The girls turned and looked at him, wide-eyed. Then they giggled and ran off.

Red-faced but determined, Freddie looked

"The mystery cat!"

around. Coming toward him was a lanky boy eating ice cream. Freddie stood in his path. "MEOW!"

The boy stopped eating. "BAA-BAAA," he replied, grinning and walked around Freddie.

Bert and Nan came over with Flossie, who had picked up her fish. "You'd better cut it out, Freddie," said his brother. "Or the zoo keeper will put you in a cage."

Just then a shrill whistle split the air and they saw Peppo running toward them. "I went to the hotel and Della told me you'd come here," he said. "How would you like some help with your detective work? I don't have to take the boat out today."

"We sure can use an interpreter," said Bert.

Freddie was staring at Peppo. "He has awfully thin arms," the boy thought, and remembered how hard Peppo had laughed at the toy mouse in the cheese jar.

Taking a deep breath, Freddie stepped up to the boy. "MEOW," he said.

Peppo laughed. "What do you want, Freddie—a bowl of milk?"

The little boy blushed. "No."

Suddenly Peppo frowned. "I think I understand. Has the mystery cat been bothering you?" he asked.

"Yes," said Nan. "Freddie's octopus is gone."

Flossie held up the red ball. "The cat left this instead." She gave it to her brother.

Peppo looked uncomfortable and said, "That's too bad."

As the children walked on, Bert said, "Peppo, I've been thinking about that light and I feel pretty sure I saw it. Do you think we could go back and look for it tonight?"

Peppo shook his head. "My boss has taken the boat on an overnight trip. Anyhow, it was probably only a fisherman you saw."

As he spoke, they strolled into a round plaza with a big splashing fountain in the center and a ring of marble statues around the edge.

Nan gasped. A man was going out the walk at the other side of the plaza. It was Gano!

Freddie opened his mouth to shout and Bert quickly clapped a hand over it.

"We must follow him," he whispered. "Don't let him see you."

Peppo snapped his fingers and beckoned them into the trees. Quietly they hurried in the direction the man was going.

Now and then they caught glimpses of the big black hat moving along, just above the bushes lining the walk. Near the gate, they gathered behind a clump of brush and watched Gano come out of the walk into the open.

A moment later he stepped through the gate

and hailed a cab. As he climbed in, the watchers rushed forward.

"Get the license number," cried Nan.

Too late. The cab slipped into the heavy boulevard traffic and was gone.

Bert heaved a great sigh of disappointment. "Come on," he said. "Let's go back to the plaza. Maybe Gano left a clue there which will help us trace him."

They trotted back and entered the circle of statues. It was empty. All was quiet except for the splash of the fountain. Suddenly a squeaky voice called, "Ha-ha-ha! I see you!"

CHAPTER XI

THE HIDDEN MESSAGE

"WHERE is that voice coming from?" asked Nan, puzzled.

The children looked around the deserted plaza.

Flossie giggled. "The statues can't talk."

Suddenly Bert pointed toward the figure of a Greek goddess on a high pedestal. Clasped around her marble waist were two small sun-browned arms.

Bert whispered something to the others and they all followed him quietly to the statue. With his hand he counted silently, *one-two-three!* Then all together the children shouted, "We see you!"

Bibi popped her head out and a huge grin split her face. She inched around to the front of the pedestal and jumped off.

"I fooled you," she said happily.

"Bibi," said Bert, "did you see Mr. Gano—the big man in the black hat?"

"Yes," said Bibi. "He's the one I tried to sell

my jar to yesterday." She skipped over to the fountain, boosted herself onto the rim of the basin and dangled her hand in the water. "Ummm, it's cool," she said, as the others followed her over.

"Bibi," said Peppo sternly, "this is serious. Did you see what Mr. Gano was doing here?"

"Start from the beginning, Bibi," said Nan, kindly.

"We-ell," said the little girl, "first I went to the hotel to play with Nan and Flossie. Della said they were over here and I came, too. I saw that man on one of the paths, so I stopped him and tried to sell him my jar again, but he didn't want it. So I ran after him and kept asking, but he got mad and yelled at me."

"Where is your jar?" Flossie asked, puzzled.

"In my black bag," said Bibi.

"Where is that?" said Flossie.

"It's around somewhere," replied Bibi, playing with the water.

"Never mind the bag," said Peppo. "Did the man meet someone here in the plaza?"

"I don't know. I was playing around and later I saw him come out. Then you chased him. When I heard you coming back, I decided to hide and play a trick on you."

Bert sighed. "All this tells us nothing about Gano."

"Maybe he came here to meet Tucci," Nan suggested.

"Or leave a note for him," said Bert. "Let's search."

As they scattered around the plaza Freddie said, "I'll look over the fountain. You can help," he added to Bibi. "Follow me."

He climbed up and began to walk around the rim. In the center were several stone dolphins with streams of water spouting from their mouths.

"What's the matter with this one?" asked Freddie. From an end Dolphin there came only a slow trickle.

"I bet something's holding the water back," said Bibi.

"That's an idea," Freddie agreed. "Maybe Gano stuck something in there."

He kneeled on the rim, leaned across the basin and rested one hand against the dolphin. With the other he reached into the open mouth.

"We're right!" he said excitedly, as his fingers closed on a hard object. He pulled and suddenly it came loose. "Aw, it's only a stone."

"Is there anything else?" asked Bibi eagerly.

As Freddie peered into the dolphin's mouth, he heard a gushing noise.

Splash! Out jetted the stream of water straight into his face.

Gasping, he heaved himself backward and jumped off the fountain rim. Bibi was laughing. Hearing the commotion, the others hurried over.

"Oh, Freddie, look at you!" said Nan.

"What have you got in your hand?" asked Bert.

"A stone," said Freddie, wiping the water from his face. "I thought it was a clue."

"Some mean person must have stuck that in the fountain for a joke," said Bibi.

Bert and Nan gave their brother clean handkerchiefs and he wiped his face and head.

Peppo said, "The sun's so hot he'll dry off in no time."

The other children went back to their search followed by Freddie and Bibi.

Nan looked carefully at the statue of a woman in Greek robes holding her hand up. At one time her fingers had curved around a staff, but now it was gone. The girl stared up at the hole where it had been.

"Look, Flossie," she said, "is there something in there?"

The little girl squinted upward. "I think so," she said.

Nan called the others, and Bert lifted his little sister onto the pedestal. Peppo found a stick and handed it to her.

Flossie poked it down into the hole as the others looked upward hopefully.

"It's a paper!" exclaimed Nan as something white dropped out. Bert made a grab and caught it. He unfolded the paper, then handed it to Peppo.

"It's in Italian."

"It's a paper!" exclaimed Nan

Peppo translated out loud:

Royal Palace at noon or here at eight tomorrow evening.

"Royal Palace!" exclaimed Flossie. "Does a queen live there?"

Peppo smiled. "Not now. But many years ago the rulers of Sicily used the palace."

"Is the note signed?" Bert asked.

Peppo shook his head. "No names on it at all."

"The paper looks clean," said Nan. "It can't have been in there too long. Maybe it's from Gano to Tucci."

Carefully Peppo folded the note and gave it to Flossie. "Put it back," he instructed. The little girl tucked the paper into the marble hand.

"We'll have to keep watch here and at the palace," said Bert.

"Why don't we call the police?" asked Freddie.

"Because we're not sure this note had anything to do with Gano and Tucci," said Bert. "We don't want to give a false alarm."

"I'll help you watch," Peppo volunteered. "But we'd better get started for the palace."

First they hurried back to the hotel to tell the Amatos.

As they walked into the lobby, a voice boomed, "Peppo!" Emilio came striding toward him, followed by Della and Uncle Mario. As they all talked in Italian, Peppo's face fell. He turned to the twins.

"My aunt is sick in Monreale," he said. "Mama had to go there, so I must play the piano for the matinee."

Emilio rolled his eyes and shuddered. "I hate to think about it." Then he winked at the children. "You have never heard such playing!"

Bibi put her hands on her hips and said to Emilio, "Peppo plays very good!"

Her two cousins laughed. "*Grazie,* Bibi," said Peppo, hugging her, "but the truth is the truth." He grinned at the Bobbseys. "They only use me in a pinch."

The brothers hurried away with Bibi tagging behind. Bert told Della about the note.

"I know the Royal Palace," she said, then glanced at the lobby clock. "We'll start now. It's nearly noon."

In their rented car, they drove through the crowded streets and up a hill to the Royal Palace, a huge pinkish building. Della parked in a paved plaza. Nearby was a line of empty tour buses. Beyond lay a garden with palm trees and a gleaming white fountain with ornate decorations.

"The place is so big," said Nan, "where shall we look for Gano and Tucci?"

Bert suggested that he and Della go into the palace while the others kept watch ouside.

"Good idea," Nan agreed.

Bert and Della went in at once and up the beautiful staircase which rose around a courtyard.

They followed a group of tourists and soon found themselves in the Palatine Chapel. Here the walls were covered with richly colored mosaic pictures. How they gleamed with gold! The two completed the tour, but saw nothing of Gano or Tucci.

Meanwhile Nan and the young twins stood near the entrance where they could watch people coming and going.

After a while one of the large tour buses pulled away, revealing the low wall which divided the plaza from the garden.

Sitting on the wall with his back to them, was a large man in a dark coat, wearing a big black hat.

"It's Gano!" exclaimed Freddie. He dashed across the plaza.

"Wait, Freddie!" Nan called.

But her brother did not look back. He gave a flying leap and landed on the man!

CHAPTER XII

A MIDNIGHT VISITOR

"NOW we've caught you!" Freddie cried, as the man gave a loud grunt. Angrily, he flung Freddie off and staggered to his feet. The black hat had fallen off and Freddie saw the man had thin gray hair.

"Oh, I'm sorry!" the boy gasped. "You're the wrong man."

Just then Nan and Flossie came racing up with Della and Bert behind them.

"I made a mistake," said Freddie unhappily.

"Yes, we saw," said Bert grimly.

Della quickly explained to the man in his own language. He listened scowling, while Nan picked up his hat and a newspaper from the grass nearby.

"We are very sorry it happened," she said earnestly.

"Say *'Scusi,'* " said Della quickly.

"Scusi," chorused the children.

107

The man accepted his hat and paper. *"Grazie."* He looked hard at Freddie, then smiled and said something to Della. He made a little bow and walked off.

Della sighed. "Freddie, he said you were a real fighter—brave as Orlando."

"But from now on," said Bert sternly, "you look before you leap."

Crestfallen, Freddie followed the others back to the car. Della waited there while Bert showed his brother and sisters the mosaics in the palace.

"It's nearly two o'clock, " she said, when they returned. "I guess Gano and Tucci aren't coming here today."

"And we won't have another chance to pick up their trail until tomorrow night," said Bert as they got into the car.

"I've been thinking about that," said Nan. "If the men *do* appear in the park, we need a quick way to get the police."

"We'll make a human chain," said Bert. "You and I will hide in the bushes so we can see into the plaza. Freddie can be hidden halfway between there and the gate, where Flossie will hide. Della, you wait on the corner across the street."

"What about Uncle Mario?" asked Nan.

"He'll be at the door of the hotel," said Bert. "As soon as we see the men, you run to tell Freddie, he races to Flossie, who signals Della."

"And I'll wave to Papa," said Della.

"Right," said Bert, "and he can call the police to come to the park."

"But what if Gano and Tucci leave before they get there?" Nan asked.

Bert looked worried. "That's the hitch. I wish we had about a dozen persons to surround them if they try to get away."

Della started the car. "There's nothing more we can do about those men today." She suggested lunch and a ride to Monreale, a village in the mountains behind Palermo.

"Oh, let's ask Bibi to go with us," said Flossie.

Della agreed and after they had eaten, they picked up the child.

Bibi looked eagerly out the window as they drove through the city, then up a winding road toward the hilltop. "I've never been to Monreale," the little girl said. "Will we see the woodcarver?"

"What woodcarver?" asked Freddie.

"The one who used to make our puppets," she answered. "Peppo told me about him. He was Grandfather Martino's special friend."

"That would be fun," said Nan. "Do you know where he lives?"

"I think I do," put in Della. "Papa took me to see his workshop when I was a little girl. His name is Alfredo."

When they reached Monreale, Della drove

along the main street and parked near a huge cathedral. She led them down a side street of small houses and paused before a yellow one with a tile roof.

"This is it," she said and knocked on the door.

After a few moments it opened and a plump woman with short black hair looked out. In Italian Della asked to see the woodcarver. The woman shook her head and replied quickly.

"Alfredo doesn't live here anymore," Della translated. "He has gone to stay with his daughter in America, but this lady doesn't know where."

As she spoke a man with a tiny mustache appeared behind the woman in the doorway.

"We used to live next door," he said in slow English, "so we knew Alfredo. Are you friends of his?"

Bibi spoke up. "No, but my Grandfather Martino was."

The man smiled. "Ah," he said, "I saw your grandfather many times. A fine old gentleman! Never will I forget the last time he came here— just two days before he died."

"He came here!" exclaimed Nan.

"Yes," said the man. "It was the day after he arrived home from Milan. How happy he was— whistling as he came up the walk!"

Bert and Nan felt a thrill of excitement. Could

the visit to the woodcarver have had anything
to do with the secret about Orlando?

"Do you know why Mr. Martino came?" Bert
asked.

"No," said the man. "He didn't bring or take
away any puppets. If you are interested in him,
or the woodcarver, you should go see my cousin.
He lived with us and knew them both. You will
find him selling postcards in front of the cathedral."

After the man described the seller, the visitors
thanked the couple and left. Among the other
souvenir sellers, they spotted the cousin. He was
a small man with baggy pants standing beside a
cart of colored postcards. Next to him was a
battered straight chair.

Della explained who they were and Nan asked
if the man had any idea why Grandfather Martino had visited the woodcarver.

The little man spread his hands wide
and shrugged. "No," he said. "Sorry I can't
help."

His eye was on a group of tourists spilling
out of the cathedral. The next moment they
had surrounded his stand and he was lost to
sight.

Disappointed, the twins and their friends
walked away. Suddenly a shrill whistle split the
air. They looked back and saw the vendor stand-

ing on his chair and waving at them over the heads of his customers.

"Come back! I'll tell you something!" he called.

As the visitors hurried to him, the tourists drifted away.

"What is it?" asked Nan eagerly.

"I almost forgot," he said. "Signor Martino came twice that day. The second time was around midnight."

"Midnight!" Nan exclaimed.

"Yes. I questioned Alfredo about it in the morning, but he wouldn't talk. And then next day he left for America."

"Tell us about Mr. Martino," said Bert eagerly. "Was he carrying anything?"

"Oh yes. A big canvas sack with something heavy in it. And he stayed in the woodcarver's house for almost two hours." The vendor smiled. "I had a toothache and couldn't sleep, so I sat by the window and watched."

"Did he have the sack when he left?" asked Bert.

"Yes, and there was still something heavy in it." He added that the old man had come in his car.

The little man smiled at the children. "Everybody knew Grandfather Martino and his dramatic tricks. It was probably some kind of joke he was fixing up."

"Come back! I'll tell you something!"

The children and Della thanked the man, then bought some postcards and left.

As they got into the car, Della said, "What do you think it all means?"

"I'll bet the heavy thing in the bag was Orlando," said Bert. "Grandfather Martino probably took the puppet to the woodcarver to have him do something to it."

"But what?"

"Who knows?" said Bert.

"And why did he go in the middle of the night?" asked Freddie.

"That's easy," said Bert. "He had to sneak Orlando out of the theater and back again without the family finding out. But first he went in the daytime to talk it over with the woodcarver."

Nan smiled. "Maybe we'll be able to learn the secret about the puppet."

Bibi bounced up and down in excitement. "I can't wait to tell Peppo!"

But on the way out of Monreale, Della stopped for a few minutes so that all the children could go into a sweet shop where Nan bought everybody candy.

She gave Bibi two small net bags of candy oranges. "I'll give one to Peppo," said Bibi.

Bert grinned. "I wonder if Danny got his present yet?" He explained the trick to Bibi.

The little girl's eyes danced. "I love jokes," she said.

Meanwhile Freddie had been buying a big bag of the oranges. "Why are you getting so much?" asked Flossie.

"I have an idea," he replied mysteriously. "I'll tell you later."

When they reached the Martinos', Papa and his sons were in the kitchen. The men were amazed at the news the children told them.

"You Bobbseys are really alert," said Peppo warmly.

Nan blushed. "It would be wonderful," she said, "if we could find Dom and Orlando and learn the secret of the King's Puppet, too."

While they were there, Bert arranged to meet Peppo at the park the next evening.

"I'll come," the boy promised, "but I must be back at the theater by nine o'clock to play for the performance."

Papa Martino invited the visitors to return with Peppo and see the show. They said they would, if their adventure in the park was over in time.

Next day the children could think of nothing except what might happen that evening. By suppertime when they gathered in the hotel dining room, they were too excited to eat much.

After Bert had reminded them all of their parts,

the younger twins announced that they had a surprise. "Bibi helped us with it," said Flossie importantly.

But the others hardly replied, for their thoughts were on the capture they hoped to make.

At half-past seven Bert stood up. "All right, everybody. Time to go to your places. Remember to be very quiet. If the men see or hear us, they'll run away."

After Freddie and Flossie had been placed, Bert and Nan hastened to the plaza. A soft whistle greeted them and Peppo's head rose above a bush beside a statue.

"If we hide here," he said, "we can see the plaza and all four of the walks which come into it."

Bert and Nan crouched down beside him. They could hear their hearts pounding as the minutes ticked by.

Suddenly shrill voices sounded ahead of them. Bert peered over the top of the brush.

About a dozen children were trooping down a path toward the plaza, laughing and talking. Leading them were the young twins and Bibi!

"Shhh! Be quiet!" Freddie called to their followers.

"*Silenzio!*" shouted Bibi, but the children kept on chattering.

At the same moment Bert spied Gano and

Tucci coming down opposite paths into the plaza.

Frantically he waved at the approaching children to go back.

"It's all right, Bert!" Flossie's voice rang out. "These are Bibi's friends. They're going to help us catch the bad men!"

CHAPTER XIII

LOST!

A SPLIT second later the children trooped into the plaza. At the same moment the two men arrived.

"There they are!" Freddie shouted to his followers. "Surround 'em!"

Bibi cried out a sharp order in Italian and the children ran screeching toward the men.

Gano turned and raced down the path as Tucci did the same in the opposite direction. Nan, Flossie, and Bibi ran after Gano with some of the children while the others chased Tucci.

The long-legged man left the path and bounded lightly ahead of them, leaping over bushes.

"Faster!" panted Peppo.

Bert sprinted ahead and soon was at Tucci's heels.

Suddenly the tall man whirled and seized Bert. He hurled the boy backward onto his pursuers.

118

As Peppo and the other leaders tumbled into a heap, Freddie shouted, "Grab him!"

Too late! Tucci gave a leap, caught an overhanging branch and swung himself up into the tree.

Peppo jumped for his feet and missed.

The searchers heard the thrashing of leaves as the man escaped overhead.

"He'll make for the gate, I bet," Bert said, scrambling up. "Come on, Freddie!"

"The rest of us will spread out around here," said Peppo.

The brothers ran to the entrance. No one was there but a gatekeeper dozing in the chair.

On the opposite corner they could see Della. She was looking over at them, puzzled.

"We'll tell her what happened," said Bert.

As they stepped through the gate, Freddie pointed up the street. "Look!" A large tree overhung the high iron fence and one of the leafy branches was shaking. A moment later Tucci dropped from the limb to the sidewalk.

As the boys sped toward him, he glanced behind. With a bound he was in the street in the midst of the fast-moving cars and motorcycles.

"He'll be hit!" Bert exclaimed.

But Tucci threaded his way expertly across the street and leaped to the curb in safety.

While the boys were crossing, the man disappeared into a narrow side street.

Panting, they followed. To their surprise, the fugitive was leaning against a house on the next corner. As soon as he saw them, he grinned slyly and sped around the corner.

The two boys chased after him and at the next corner, saw him waiting again beside a small fountain. Time after time they saw him, but his long legs kept him easily out of their reach.

At first the boys did not notice the streets were becoming narrower and more deserted.

Suddenly they rounded a bend and found themselves in a short dead-end street. Ahead was a blank wall. Houses with shuttered windows rose on either side.

"Did he go this way?" Freddie asked.

Bert shrugged. "I didn't see. He might have cut down some other street. I think he was trying to get us lost."

"Should we knock on all the doors and ask for Tucci?" asked Freddie doubtfully.

Bert shook his head. "If he is hiding here, you don't think anybody would tell us, do you?" He was still cross with his brother for breaking up the capture plans.

Feeling very guilty, Freddie said no more.

"What's the name of this street?" Bert asked. "Maybe the police could search here for Tucci."

The boys had noticed that Italian street names were often painted on the wall of the corner building. In the fading light they peered at the peeling paint.

"All I can make out is *Via*," said Bert. "That's a big help! It means street."

"Maybe we could bring the police here," suggested Freddie.

"We'll be lucky if we get out ourselves," said Bert. He thought of the many twists and turns they had taken and his heart sank. It was dusk now and for sometime they had seen no one on the streets. Nor had there been any vehicles, not even a bicycle. All was silent. Bert reached into his pocket and brought out his small map of Palermo.

"We're lost," Freddie quavered, "and it's all my fault."

Bert patted his brother's shoulder. "We'll find our way out," he said, consulting the map.

"I'm sorry about everything," Freddie went on. "When you wished for enough helpers to surround the men, I got the idea to hire some policemen of our own. We paid 'em with all those candy oranges I bought. I thought you could show them where to hide and then Flossie and I would go back to our posts."

Bert nodded. "It might have worked, too, Freddie," he admitted, "if only Gano and Tucci hadn't showed up early."

"I wanted to make up for jumping on the man

in the park," said Freddie unhappily, "but I made everything worse."

"No use worrying about it," said Bert kindly. "Even if we knew the name of the street, this map wouldn't help us," he added, putting it in his pocket. "These old streets aren't on it. Besides, it's too dark to see the printing."

"What'll we do?" asked Freddie.

"Keep going," said Bert. "Sooner or later we ought to hit a main street."

The brothers started off again. Now and then they came to a pool of light beneath a street lamp, but mostly they walked in darkness.

Suddenly Bert stopped and said, "Listen!" In the distance they could hear music. The boys hurried toward the sound.

As they drew closer Freddie exclaimed, "Automobile horns, too! Hear 'em?"

The noises became louder and as they turned a corner they suddenly found themselves on a brightly lighted street crowded with cars and people. From the open door of a record shop blared a popular song.

"Thank goodness!" exclaimed Bert. "From here we can get back to the hotel."

"Maybe the others caught Gano," said Freddie hopefully, as his brother flagged a taxi.

Gano had sped around the park paths with the children pounding after him until they were dizzy.

"We're lost," Freddie quavered

Suddenly Bibi called, "Where did he go?"

"Straight ahead, I think," Nan cried

The others raced onward, but Flossie spotted a bush moving behind a rickety-looking bench.

"He's hiding. I bet," she thought. She tiptoed to the bench and climbed onto it. Quietly she parted the bushes and looked down into them. With a flap of wings a bird flew out. Startled, Flossie jumped sideways.

"Crack! The wood broke and Flossie's foot went down between two slats. "Help!" she called. "Nan!"

After a few minutes her shrill cries reached her sister's ears and Nan came running back.

"Floss! What happened?"

"My foot's stuck," said Flossie. As Nan tried to get it loose, the little girl explained how it had happened.

"Let's take your shoe off," said Nan. Quickly she reached under the bench and removed Flossie's sandal. "Now try."

But the sharp splinters made it impossible to work the foot up.

Nan sighed. "If you and Freddie had stuck to your posts," she said sternly, "this might never have happened."

Flossie's eyes filled with tears and a big one rolled off her nose. "I know," she wept. "We spoiled everything."

Nan's face softened. "There now, don't cry. Let's get you out of here."

But no matter how Nan turned and twisted her sister's foot, she could not get it through the hole.

She was hardly aware that the shadows had lengthened and the cries of the other children had long since stopped. Suddenly a bell rang loudly.

"What's that?" asked Flossie.

"I don't know," said Nan. She sat back on her heels with a sigh. "I'll have to break all those splinters off the boards."

It was a prickly job and by the time she had finished, it was dark. In the distance the girls heard the lion roar.

Flossie shivered. "I wish we were home in the hotel."

"Try again, Floss."

This time the little girl gave a squeak of pain, but the foot was squeezed through the slats.

"Oh, Nan, I love you!" she exclaimed and stepped off the bench. Flossie put on her shoe and stepped on the foot. "It's all right," she said. "Let's go now. This park is scary."

Hand in hand the two hurried down the path. As they reached the big gate, they saw it was closed.

Together they pushed hard on it, but the iron bars did not move. They were locked in!

CHAPTER XIV

THE WRONG HEAD

"HELP!" Nan called through the bars of the gate. At that moment a young man and woman came around the corner.

"We're locked in!" cried Flossie.

The couple stopped and stared. Then they asked questions in Italian. When the girls could not answer, the man hurried away. The woman reached in and patted Flossie's head kindly as several other passersby paused and asked more questions.

Soon the man came hurrying back with the gatekeeper, who was carrying a large key on a ring. Quickly he unlocked the gate and pulled it open.

"Oh *grazie!*" exclaimed the girls as they stepped through to freedom.

The keeper shook his finger at them and scolded in Italian. He reached up, pulled an imaginary rope, and cried, "Ding-dong! Ding-dong!"

"Oh, the bell!" Nan exclaimed. "It was the signal that the park was closing! We're so sorry to have made trouble for you," she added.

"*Scusi*," piped up Flossie.

The bystanders smiled and the gatekeeper nodded. "*Si, si,*" he said and locked the gate again.

As the other people moved off, the young couple offered in sign language to take the girls home.

Nan pointed to the hotel and said, "We can go ourselves." But the strangers insisted on walking the children to the door. The girls thanked them and as the couple left, a taxi drew up. Out hopped the boys. Bert paid the driver and all the twins hurried into the lobby.

Della and Mr. Amato jumped up from their chairs to meet them. "Where have you been? What happened?" Uncle Mario asked.

"We were getting ready to call the police." said Della.

Quickly the children told their stories. Della added that she had tried to follow Bert and Freddie but had lost them. "I decided I'd better come back and report to Papa."

"What about Gano?" Bert asked anxiously.

"Just as I reached the corner again," said Della, "he came dashing out the gate, hopped into a cab, and was gone. Peppo and Bibi ran out a few moments later followed by a lot of children." She looked puzzled. "Who were all those others?"

Freddie and Flossie grew pink. Nan spoke up quickly. "Friends of Bibi. They were trying to help us, but it didn't work."

Bert sighed. "One thing's sure. Gano and Tucci will never meet in that park again."

"What about the dead-end street where you thought Tucci might have hidden in a house?" Nan asked.

"There are plenty of old streets like that," Della said, frowning. "If the boys don't know the name, it's hopeless."

"Now that we've lost Gano and Tucci," said Nan, "how will we ever find Dom and the puppet?"

"We still have one clue," said Bert, "the *Red Eye*. If we could only locate that boat!"

Mr. Amato sat up straight and snapped his fingers. "I know what to do! Bert, my boy, we'll hire a plane first thing in the morning and you, Nan, and I will search the coast from the air."

"That's a wonderful idea!" exclaimed Bert, and the others agreed excitedly.

The little man jumped up. "We'll spy out those rascals! They won't get away! I'll make arrangements right this minute!" He bustled off to talk to the desk clerk.

Della glanced at her watch. "Go to your rooms

and freshen up quickly," she said to the twins. "We just have time to make the puppet performance."

When they reached the little theater, Peppo was standing outside the red curtains and waved them through.

"We're ready to begin," he said. "Sit on the front bench."

The theater was lighted by a single bright bulb and crowded with people laughing and talking.

The visitors took their seats, facing an upright piano at the foot of the stage.

"What a nice curtain!" exclaimed Flossie. On it was a faded painting of knights on chargers. For the first time there was enough light for the Bobbseys to get a good look at the walls.

"They're hung with stage scenery," remarked Nan. As she admired the painted castles, gardens and forests, Bibi slipped onto the bench beside her.

"Those are old drops we can't use any more," she said and squeezed Nan's hand. "I can hardly wait to see the show tonight!"

Just then the light went out and there was a loud knock on wood from backstage. The audience grew quiet.

"That's Papa Martino stamping on the floor," Della whispered. "It's Peppo's cue to start the music."

As she spoke, the boy came running down the

center aisle, swung himself onto the piano bench and banged out a chord. The curtain jerked up. Several puppets clanked onto the stage, and Papa Martino's voice roared out as he spoke first for one, then another. Soon swords rang against shields and heads flew off as the battle raged hotter.

"Oh, it's great!" cried Freddie as the audience clapped and cheered for their favorite knights.

At the end of each scene, the curtain fell and Peppo played loudly, skipping some of the notes.

Flossie looked around at the audience. "Everybody's having so much fun," she said.

"People in Sicily love the paladin plays," Della told her, "and know all the characters."

A little later a knight strode onto the stage in silvery armor and a yellow brass helmet. Excited cries and laughter broke from the house. Bibi began to giggle.

Peppo looked up at the stage. "Oh, no!" he exclaimed. He turned around, bursting into laughter. "That puppet has the wrong head on!"

The curtain fell. Clanking noises could be heard backstage and angry voices. A loud stamp sounded.

"Play, Peppo," said Della. But he was laughing too hard.

Quickly Nan slipped to the piano bench and began to play *The Stars and Stripes Forever*.

The audience cheered and whistled. Suddenly the stamping noise came from backstage and Nan

"That puppet has the wrong head!"

stopped the music. The curtain jerked up, revealing the same puppet with a silver-colored head and body. Loud applause greeted him and the performance went on.

When it was over, the visitors went backstage with Peppo and Bibi.

Papa Martino took Nan's hand. "I was looking out and saw you playing," he said. "We owe you thanks."

Nan smiled. "I played the loudest piece I knew."

"And you, Peppo," said his father sternly, "why did you forget your duty?"

"I'm sorry, Papa. I was laughing so hard I couldn't help it."

"It wasn't funny back here," declared Emilio. "I took a head off the shelf, put it on the puppet, and moved him onto the stage. The light was dim and I was in a hurry, so I didn't notice it was the wrong head."

Stefano explained that the heads were lined up in the order they were to be used.

"They were all right when I checked this afternoon, but somebody switched two of them. Now who would do that?"

No one spoke up.

"It's the kind of trick the mystery cat plays," said Bert. "Maybe he's the one."

Vince shook his head. "If I ever catch that cat, I'll give him something to meow about!"

Peppo bit back a grin. As his brothers began

to clear the stage of puppets, he went to the switchboard and turned out the footlights.

Bert followed him and said, "Peppo, do you know who the mystery cat is?"

The Sicilian's dark eyes sparkled. "Why ask me?"

"If the joke goes on much longer, there'll be a lot of people mad at him," Bert said. "I'd hate to see anybody I like get into trouble."

"I would, too," Peppo admitted. "But I think the tricks are funny."

"Maybe you ought to warn the person to stop— if you know who it is, I mean."

Peppo grinned, "Well, *if* I do, *maybe* I will." He slapped Bert on the shoulder and walked off.

On the way home Bert told the others what he and Peppo had said to each other.

"I think he's the cat himself," declared Freddie.

"Or else he knows who it is," said Nan.

As she spoke they stepped into a deserted street lit by a single light hanging from a wall. At the far end was an ornate stone arch, leading to the boulevard.

"That used to be the carriage gateway to a palace," said Uncle Mario.

"It's that big old building near the arch," said Della. "You've passed it before."

When they reached the palace, the children paused to look up. The whole end wall was gone. Inside, all was dark.

"What happened to it, Uncle Mario?" Flossie asked.

"It was partly blown up," he replied. "Sicily has been the scene of many battles. The palace has been this way for years."

As they gazed into the gaping ruin, there came a soft meow.

Nan stiffened. Had something moved in the deep shadows of the yard? A moment later the sound came again, going toward the palace.

"It might be the mystery cat," whispered Flossie excitedly.

"Let's find out," urged Nan. "May we, Uncle Mario?"

"You and Bert go," he replied. "But I say it's only a cat—a four-legged one. Here," he added, "take my pocket flashlight."

The older twins picked their way across the rubble-filled yard and stepped into the ruin. Bert beamed the light around the high-ceilinged room. It was empty.

They moved on through a broken wall to the foot of a wide marble staircase. From the dark gallery above them came a low meow.

Quietly the twins ran up and Bert flashed the light around. Nothing there.

The children stepped through a door into a huge salon. At the far end, where the wall was missing, they could see the stars. There was no furniture except a stone chest against one wall.

On the other side loomed a fireplace with a yawning black hole big enough to hold half a dozen men.

"*Meow-ow!*" The sound came from that hole.

Nan held her breath as Bert beamed his light into it. Near the floor gleamed two green eyes!

"A real cat!" the twins exclaimed. As they laughed, it darted away into the darkness.

"Let's tell the others," said Nan. They picked their way over the broken tile floor to the open side of the room.

But as Nan stepped to the edge to call out, a tile slipped from under her foot. With a cry she pitched forward and began to fall toward the yard below.

CHAPTER XV

A FISHERMAN'S CLUE

QUICKLY Bert seized Nan's arm and jerked her back to safety. The tile fell over the edge and broke on the rubble two stories below.

"Oh, thanks!" gasped Nan. "That was close!"

Anxious calls came from the group on the sidewalk. "She's all right!" shouted Bert.

"But my knees are still shaking," said Nan as they made their way toward the marble staircase.

Outside, Bert reported finding a real cat.

"I was hoping you'd catch the mystery cat," said Freddie, disappointed.

"So were we," said Bert, "but it's more important to rescue Dom and Orlando."

"There's a double mystery about that puppet," remarked Nan. "We don't know where he's being held or what the secret about him is."

Next morning at breakfast, Flossie asked if she and Freddie could play with Bibi.

"Good idea," said Della. "I'll go with you and visit Aunt Bartolina."

"I wish we could all ride in the airplane," said Freddie.

"So do I," replied Uncle Mario kindly, "but there's not enough room."

"I hope you have good luck this time," remarked Della. "We've come so close to catching Gano and Tucci, but something always goes wrong."

She did not notice that Freddie and Flossie stole sheepish looks at each other. But Nan saw them. "They still feel bad about spoiling our plan," she thought.

Half an hour later Uncle Mario was at the wheel of the car with the older twins beside him. A hot breeze whipped their faces as they drove along the seacoast. Suddenly Bert pointed out several small brightly colored planes on a field beside the water.

"That's where we're going," said Uncle Mario. "It's a private airport."

He swung onto a dirt road and drove down to the landing field. As he parked, they were met by a handsome young man wearing a white shirt and blue slacks.

"I am Pietro Cassino, your pilot," he said in careful English. "You may call me Pete."

He led them to a silver seaplane moored at a dock. The passengers climbed inside and the children buckled themselves into two seats behind Pete and Uncle Mario.

As the motors roared, the plane scudded across the water and soared into the air. While Uncle Mario explained their mission to the pilot, the twins watched the blue sea sparkling below.

Pete flew low, and they had a good look at the brown cliffs along the shore. Now and then the children spotted small beaches and coves. Scattered over the water were fishing boats and motor launches with bright-colored canopies, but they saw no yellow boat with a red eye.

Suddenly Nan called, "Look!" Drawn up in a sandy cove was a large yellow fishing boat. Nearby, in the shade of a rock, sat a man mending a net.

"That's not Vito or Tucci," said Bert, "and there's no red eye on the boat."

"They could have painted over it for a disguise," said Nan.

"Let's go down and take a look," said Uncle Mario.

Skillfully Pete set the seaplane down and taxied toward the boat. All its paint was old and worn.

"Wrong one," said Bert.

The fisherman stood up and stared at their craft suspiciously. He was a stocky man with curly black hair.

"Let's go ashore and talk to him anyway," Nan

suggested. "Maybe he would know where the *Red Eye* is."

"You'll have to wade," said Pete. "I can't get any closer."

Quickly the passengers took off their shoes and slipped into the water. Moments later the cool foam had given way to burning sand.

"Ouch!" muttered Nan as they picked their way toward the fisherman. He stood with his hands on his hips beside his net, watching them come. At his feet was a large basket of fish.

"He doesn't look so friendly," remarked Bert softly.

"Uncle Mario," said Nan, "tell him we're friends and that we're looking for Tucci and the *Red Eye*."

At this, the fisherman scowled and spoke threateningly to Uncle Mario. The little man walked up to him bravely and replied, but the Sicilian shouted louder, pointing toward the seaplane.

"He's ordering us off!" exclaimed Bert.

Suddenly the man reached into his basket and brought up a big fish by the tail. With a roar he swung it toward Uncle Mario.

Bert seized his arm. "No, no! We're friends!" he cried.

As the fisherman tried to fling the boy off, Pete came splashing ashore, shouting.

He ran up to them and all three men talked

loudly at once. Suddenly the fisherman's eyes grew wide. He dropped the fish and smiled. Then he wiped his hands on his shirt and shook hands cordially with Uncle Mario, Pete, Bert, and Nan.

Uncle Mario gave a sigh of relief. "It was a mistake," he explained to the twins. "This man understands only a little English. He heard Nan say something about friends and Tucci. He thought we were that scoundrel's friends."

"He knows him then!" exclaimed Nan eagerly.

"Yes," said Pete. "This fellow says all the fishermen around here do. Tucci is a thief and a troublemaker. They know he lives in a village on the mainland, where everyone is afraid of him."

"That's true," said Nan.

"He comes over here in his boat, steals fish and nets, and then runs off. Because of Tucci, the fishermen have become suspicious of all strangers."

"Has anyone seen the *Red Eye* lately?" Bert asked eagerly.

Uncle Mario spoke Italian to the man, who nodded.

"*Si.*" Talking rapidly, he pointed down the coast toward a high cliff jutting into the sea.

Pete translated. "He saw Tucci's boat going toward that headland yesterday, but he doesn't know where the *Red Eye* is kept. There are lots of coves around here. He says he'll watch and if

"No, no! We're friends!"

he sees it, he'll radio me at the airport. He has a wireless on his boat."

They all thanked the fisherman and hurried back to the seaplane. As it took off, the man waved and the twins waved back.

Pete made for the headland and flew round it. Suddenly Bert recognized the shape.

"This is the promontory where I thought I saw the light in the grotto," he said to Nan.

Twice Pete flew around the headland and up and down the coast on either side of it. The only break in the cliff was a small beach. A long wooden stair rose from it to a little villa high among the rocks. But there was no sign of people or boats.

"Does anybody live on that headland?" Bert asked.

"There are a few vacation houses," Pete replied, "and only one road, which comes up from the inland side. It's a favorite place for motorcycle riders. There's so little traffic they can zoom around as fast as they want. Sometimes the cyclists camp up there."

Nan noticed a ledge which rose from the beach and ran along the middle of the headland. Above it the cliff sloped and was patched with grass.

For several hours more the searchers skycruised until their eyes were dazzled by sun and water.

"I'm afraid it's no use looking longer," said Mr. Amato. "The boat must be out at sea."

"But it may come back," said Bert. "We should try again."

"We will," Uncle Mario promised.

When they landed at the airport, the passengers followed the pilot into a small white building which was the office and shop. Nan paused before a counter of souvenirs.

"Oh, how darling!" she exclaimed, pointing to a row of little yellow Sicilian carts with brightly painted pictures on them. To each was harnessed a wooden horse wearing many-colored feather plumes on its head and back. Nan bought three carts.

"Two for Freddie and Flossie to cheer them up," she told Bert. "The other one's for Bibi."

When the twins and Uncle Mario reached the hotel, they were hungry and enjoyed a lunch of cheese and fresh-baked rolls with cool milk.

Afterward Bert and Nan walked to Aunt Bartolina's house, taking the new toys. When Flossie saw hers, she hugged Nan and said, "It's just bee-yoo-ti-ful!"

"Thanks! It's keen!" said Freddie as he admired the glittering harness on the horse.

"Where's Bibi?" asked Nan.

"She went home all of a sudden," said Flossie. "I don't know why. I hope she isn't mad at me."

"We'll find out," said Nan. "Let's take her cart over to her."

Flossie skipped across the street next to her sister and they entered the theater.

After the bright sunlight, the auditorium was pitch black. Making their way down the aisle, the girls heard a board creak backstage.

They stopped and listened.

"Meow-ow!"

"The mystery cat!" Flossie whispered.

Nan had an idea. She squeezed Flossie's hand as a signal. Then she said loudly, "Let's leave this toy on the stage and go find the boys. We can come back for it later."

The sisters felt their way to the front of the theater. Nan reached over the footlights and placed the cart on the boards. She could not feel the curtain and guessed it was up. Then the two tiptoed through the side door and up the stairs to the switchboard.

Again the floor creaked. Their eyes were becoming used to the darkness and they could make out a figure moving on the stage.

Nan's fingers fumbled over the board. She threw a switch.

There in a yellow spotlight stood Bibi!

CHAPTER XVI

THE BLACK BAG

"BIBI!" Flossie exclaimed. "You're the mystery cat!"

Startled, Bibi whirled. She stood blinking in the spotlight, a bag of candy oranges in one hand and the little cart in the other.

Then she gave a sheepish grin and walked over to the girls. "It was all a joke," she said. "See?" She held up the bag of candy. "I always leave something in exchange."

"We know you didn't mean any harm," said Nan, "but people don't like it when they need a thing and find something else there instead."

"Like the heads last night," said Flossie.

Bibi nodded. "I know." She chuckled. "I decided to do it again tonight. That's why I came here. When I heard you I gave my signal just for fun."

"You mean you've switched the heads again?" Nan asked.

"No. You came before I had time."

Flossie's eyes were as wide as saucers. "I never thought it was you, Bibi. I felt sure it was Peppo."

Bibi laughed. "He knew about me, but he wouldn't give me away." She looked worried. "Are you going to tell?"

Nan and Flossie exchanged looks.

"Everybody's mad at me," said Bibi, "but I always meant to give everything back. Only it was such fun I hated to stop. Please don't tell on me," she begged. "I promise I'll return everything now. And I'll put a candy orange with each one for good measure."

Flossie and Nan looked at each other again and nodded. "All right," said Nan, "but you must let us tell Bert and Freddie. We promise they won't give your secret away."

"Okay," said Bibi. She handed Nan the little cart. "I'll start with this."

Nan smiled. "No, that's yours. It's a present from me."

The little girl's face lit up. "Oh, thank you! Isn't it darling!" She hugged the little cart, then gave Nan a kiss.

"Come on," said Bibi, "I'll show you my hiding place."

Nan turned out the spotlight and the three girls made their way out of the theater. Bibi led them down the boulevard and past the hotel.

"How far is it?" asked Flossie.

"You'll see," said Bibi, enjoying her secret.

She went into the park to the plaza and skipped over to the statue where they had found her hiding.

Bibi crooked her finger for them to follow and crawled under a big bush behind the marble pedestal. The thick green branches arched over their heads and came down to the ground all around them.

"Why, it's like a little house in here," said Flossie.

Bibi nodded. "It's a very secret place." She lifted a bunch of twigs, reached into a shallow hole and pulled out a black cloth bag.

From it she took the purple octopus, two black stockings, a little bag of ground cheese, an old hat, and half a dozen other odd objects. On each was fastened a piece of paper with a name written in pencil.

"That's so I wouldn't forget who to give 'em back to," she explained.

Bibi felt in the bag again and brought out a small card. "Mr. Gano dropped this in the plaza the day I tried to sell him my jar," she said. "I wanted to give it back to him, but he hurried away when I called him."

"What does it say?" asked Nan.

"Donna's Pottery Shop," the child replied, "with the address and phone number."

"That's the store where we bought our fish!" Nan said.

"And Freddie saw the black hat," Flossie chimed in.

"It's a wonderful clue!" exclaimed Nan. "If we watch the place maybe we can catch Gano there!"

"You mean I helped you?" Bibi asked.

Nan hugged her. "You certainly did!"

"Do you have any other clues in your bag?" Flossie asked.

Bibi felt inside. "There's nothing left except my jar."

"Come on, then," said Nan. "We must tell the others. May I keep the card, Bibi?"

"Sure you can!" She handed the octopus to Flossie and put the other things into the bag.

The children crawled out and raced back to Aunt Bartolina's house. At the door Bibi slipped away with a wave, carrying her black bag.

"I hope she doesn't get caught giving all that stuff back," Flossie said.

The girls stepped through the bead curtain, but found no one inside. There was a note on the table telling them to go to the Martinos'.

The two girls ran across the street, went through the theater and knocked on the kitchen door.

It was opened by Mama Martino.

"Aha!" she exclaimed and gave each girl a huge hug. Sitting around the big table, talking, were all the Martinos, Della, Aunt Bartolina, and the boys.

"It's a wonderful clue!" said Nan

"My sister is well again," boomed Mama Martino, "and how glad I am to be home!" She looked at the girls' flushed faces. "What's the matter? You have fever?"

She laid a hand on Nan's brow.

"No, no!" said Flossie. "We have a clue!"

Without giving away Bibi's secret, the girls reported what she had found.

Bert examined the card. "We ought to go to this place right away," he said, jumping up.

Papa Martino raised his hand. "No use," he said. "It will be closed by the time you get there."

"We'll go first thing tomorrow," said Peppo.

Excited at the new lead, the Bobbseys and Della hurried to the hotel. On the way Flossie gave the octopus to Freddie, and Nan quietly told the boys the story of the mystery cat.

When they stopped at the desk for the key, the clerk handed Nan a letter.

"Airmail," she said and looked at the return address. "From Nellie."

Eagerly the others clustered around as she opened the envelope and read the note aloud:

"Dear Nan: All of us in the neighborhood want to thank you for the darling sugar donkeys. But poor Danny! When he saw the little box you sent him, he figured it just couldn't be fruit. He told everybody you were playing a trick on him and it was some-

thing that might blow up. So he soaked it in
water and all the candy melted. Was he mad!

> Love,
> Nellie"

The Bobbseys burst into laughter.

"Poor old Danny!" said Nan. "I can just see
his face when he opened that box!"

"He really played a trick on himself," Bert
remarked, "just because he thinks everyone is as
mean as he is."

Freddie grinned. "It must have been a mess!"

"I feel kind of sorry for him," said Flossie.
"Let's send him something else. Maybe he's
learned his lesson."

The others agreed and after supper they walked
to a sweet shop and had a bag of candy lemons
sent to Danny.

Early next morning, Peppo and Bibi were
waiting for the Bobbseys when they came down
to the lobby. The little girl was carrying her black
bag.

"Everything's back," she announced, rolling
her eyes, "—if you know what I mean."

The others grinned.

"What's in the bag, then?" asked Nan as they
left the hotel.

"My jar. I'm going to ask the pottery lady to
buy it. She could fix the crack and sell it to somebody."

When they reached the shop, Bert showed Signora Donna the card and told her of their mission.

"Gano a kidnapper!" she exclaimed. Her eyes grew round with fright. English words failed her. She spoke rapidly in Italian.

"We'll have to work quickly," Peppo translated. "Gano's coming here any minute now." He told them that the man had been trying to force Signora Donna to sell him her business for almost nothing. "He threatened to wreck the shop if she went to the police."

"Do you know where Gano could be holding Dom or why he kidnapped him?" Bert said to Signora Donna.

"No, no," she replied.

"That was his hat I saw here, wasn't it?" asked Freddie.

The woman nodded. "He saw you coming and made me promise not to tell he was here. He hid in a closet, but left his hat out by mistake."

"Come on," said Bert anxiously. "We'll hide till he comes."

The others followed him across the street and into a narrow alley.

"Nan," said Bert, "you run for a policeman."

She raced away. A few moments later Gano, wearing his black hat, strode through the shop door.

"Now!" said Bert. "Let's go!"

The children hurried across the street and into the store.

Gano whirled.

Quickly Bert shut the door behind him and the children gathered solidly in front of it.

"Now, Mr. Gano, where is Dom?" asked Bert.

The man's black eyes were hard as stone. "I don't know what you mean. Go away."

"Not till you answer the question," said Peppo firmly.

The man snorted. "You'll have a long wait."

Bibi spoke up. "Well, meantime maybe somebody would like to buy my jar. I won't charge much." She looked pleadingly at Signora Donna, but the woman was too frightened to speak.

Bibi plucked Gano's sleeve. "Would you—"

"Bah!" he exploded and struck her arm away. The next instant he dashed into the kiln room. Bert and Peppo sprinted after him. He burst through the back door of the shop and down a narrow alley with the boys close behind.

Suddenly his hat blew off. A moment later he darted through a doorway and jumped down two stairs into a little courtyard.

Bert leaped off the top step and grabbed the man's thick hair. With a twist Gano shot free. But Bert still had the hair in his hand! It was a wig! The man was bald! As he dashed up a staircase across the courtyard, he looked back.

It was Carlo Vito!

CHAPTER XVII

THE EMERALD GROTTO

"CATCH him!" cried Peppo as he and Bert dashed across the courtyard. Up the stairs they sprinted behind the fleeing man.

Suddenly, on a landing Vito opened a door, darted inside, and slammed it after him. The key turned in the lock.

"Open this door!" Bert shouted, and both boys pounded. They rattled the knob and called, but no one answered. Above them doors opened and several women called down questions.

"Peppo," said Bert, "run back to the shop and bring Nan and the police. I'll watch here."

Peppo leaped down the stairs two at a time and vanished into the street. As Bert waited he heard the doors above him shut, one by one, and at last he was alone. Not a sound came from the apartment before him.

"I can guess why Dom was kidnapped," Bert

154

thought. "Vito wants to make him tell the ice cream secret."

After a while Peppo dashed in followed by Nan and a policeman. The officer knocked firmly on the door, and announced himself in Italian.

A moment later the key turned and the door opened. A thin-faced woman in a print house-dress peered out.

As the officer questioned her sharply, Peppo quietly translated: "Gano burst in on her, and kept her from opening the door. Just a few minutes ago he slipped out the back way."

Bert frowned. "I was afraid of that."

The officer then thanked the children for the tip. He was surprised to know that Gano was really Vito.

"It explains how he left that restaurant without the police noticing him," Bert said. "He must have taken off his wig and mustache and walked out as Vito."

The officer agreed and asked them to keep on the lookout for the big man and Tucci.

Nan was amazed at Vito's disguise. On the way back to Donna's shop, the twins told Peppo about the man who had eavesdropped outside the curtain at the Amato shop.

"It must have been Vito," Nan said. "He probably heard Uncle Mario say that Dom knew the ice cream recipe."

"But how could he know Dom had gone to Naples?" Peppo asked.

"We don't know—yet," replied Bert.

At the shop they found the three younger children helping Signora Donna put new pottery on the shelves.

The woman was pale-faced and nervous. "Be careful," she warned as they left the shop. "Gano is a very dangerous man."

"What are we going to do now?" asked Flossie as they started down the street.

"Have lunch, I hope," said Freddie.

"Good idea," Bert agreed. "I'll treat everybody to pizza and milk while we make our plans."

Peppo led them to a narrow shop on a side street. They stepped through the bead curtain and seated themselves at a cool white-topped table. An electric fan in the corner ruffled the girls' hair as Bibi put her black bag on the table.

"I asked the pottery lady if she would like to look at my jar, but she was too upset. Would you like to see it?" she asked, reaching into the bag.

"Some other time, dear," said Nan. "We have important things to talk about now."

Bibi sighed and put her bag on the floor.

After their orders had been given to a young girl in a white apron, Nan said, "I've been thinking about the light Bert said he saw in the grotto. If fishermen made it, where was their boat? We looked around there that night and didn't see any."

"That's true," said Bert. "And the cliff is so sheer they could not have climbed down into the cave."

"Maybe they came in a rowboat small enough to take inside with them," said Peppo.

"But it would be too far to row from Palermo," protested Nan, "and we saw only one beach near there. There was no sign of a boat on it."

"That's true," said Peppo. "What are you getting at, Nan?"

"I bet I know," said Bert. "The fisherman we met said he had seen the *Red Eye* going toward that promontory where I spotted the light. Maybe Dom is a prisoner in the grotto and it was his light we saw."

"Tucci could have taken him there in the *Red Eye*, rowed him into the grotto, and then taken both boats away," Nan added.

Peppo's face lit with excitement. "It's worth looking into."

"How about the motorboat?" Bert asked. "Can you get it this afternoon?"

"Yes," said their friend. "It's not in use today. Right after we eat, I'll make arrangements."

"We'll meet you at the dock at one o'clock," said Nan, "if Uncle Mario and Della say it's all right."

The twins found the Amatos in the hotel garden, and eagerly told their idea.

Della shook her head doubtfully. "It sounds like a wild goose chase to me. Are you absolutely sure you saw the light, Bert?"

"Yes," Bert replied firmly.

"It was probably made by a fisherman," said Mr. Amato.

He and Della looked at the twins' pleading faces. "All right." Uncle Mario gave in. "Run along, but *if* you should find any trace of Dom, you come back at once for help. Understand?"

The children promised. Then Nan and Flossie changed into pedal pushers and the boys put on shorts. They hurried to the waterfront where they found Peppo waiting in the boat.

"There was no room for Bibi," he said as he started the motor. "She was disappointed, but she knows it's Freddie and Flossie's turn. She went last time."

The midafternoon sun was hot as they rounded the promontory. They passed several low openings in the rock, then one some distance away.

"That's the grotto," said Bert. "I remember it was about here."

Peppo cut the motor, and they drifted close to the dark mouth of the cave.

"This boat's too big to go in," said Peppo softly.

"I know," said Bert, kicking off his shoes. "Nan

and I'll swim. If Dom's in there we'll bring him out."

"What if the men are with him?" Flossie whispered.

"We'll have to take that chance," said Nan.

With hardly a splash, the twins dived over the side and came up in a cool dim cavern. At one side was a rocky ledge running back into the shadows. There was no one in sight.

Bert and Nan swam a few strokes, then glanced back toward the cave mouth.

Both gasped. When they faced the light, the water was a clear brilliant green! As they moved, trails of bubbles shimmered in their wake.

"It's an emerald grotto," Nan thought.

A moment later both twins spotted a figure in a niche just above the ledge. It was Orlando!

Their hunch had been right!

"Dom!" Bert called.

"Here," came a voice. "In the back."

Swiftly the twins swam to the ledge and climbed onto it. Dripping, they made their way to an alcove. Light glimmered through a crack in the rocks high above. In a corner sat Dom, bound hand and foot!

"Bert! Nan!" he exclaimed. "Am I glad to see you!" While they exchanged excited greetings, the twins untied him.

"Is Orlando in the niche?" Dom asked anxiously.

It was Orlando!

"Yes," said Bert.

"With his armor?"

"Yes. How did he get there?" The twins noticed the empty duffel bag beside Dom.

"Gano and Tucci told me they put Orlando in the niche and sold his armor. They said if I tried to give them trouble, they would knock him into the water. From the time they kidnapped me, they've threatened Orlando in order to keep me in line."

"How mean they are!" exclaimed Nan.

"Let's get out of here now," said Bert. "You can swim, can't you, Dom?"

"Yes. But I'd be afraid to take Orlando for a dip. He's too old. His wood might warp or his paint peel off."

"Then we'll come back for him with a rowboat," said Bert.

"But if the men arrive before we do and find me gone, they'll steal him. I've got to stay."

"Okay," said Bert. "We'll send Peppo and the twins for help. They can bring back a rowboat."

"You'd better go with them," said Dom anxiously. "It's not safe for you here."

"We'll stay," said Nan firmly. "If the men come back you may need help."

Bert swam out with the message and returned with a waterproof flashlight. "Peppo had this in the boat. We might have use for it."

"I want to see Orlando," said Dom. He led

the way to the niche and looked the puppet over quickly. He sighed with relief. "I guess he's okay."

Nan then told what the twins had learned about Grandfather Martino's visit to the woodcarver.

"I've been wondering if maybe Mr. Martino had Alfredo hollow out the body and put something inside," Nan said.

"You mean some kind of treasure?" Bert added.

Dom shrugged and said they'd have to take the marionette apart to find out. "We can't do that now."

Nan looked at the puppet and shook her head. "If only you could talk, Orlando. Poor fellow," she added, "I hope you're not rusty from standing in this damp grotto."

"He's all right," said Dom. "Aren't you, old boy?" He picked up the puppet and gave him a hard playful shake.

The next moment a deep voice said, "My dear children, I have a surprise for you."

It was the puppet speaking!

The youngsters stood speechless with amazement.

Bert gulped. "A recording! That's the treasure!"

"I think it's Grandfather Martino's voice," whispered Dom. "I sort of remember it."

"He said he had a surprise," said Nan excitedly, "so there must be more to the message!"

They waited. Orlando stood silent. Bert and Dom shook the puppet hard, but it did not speak. Again and again they tried. Not a word came.

"That did it," said Bert disgustedly. "We broke the mechanism by shaking it."

Dom shook his head. "No. There must be a loose switch somewhere. It works sometimes and then again not. I'll bet it got jarred out of whack when Freddie fell off the chair with Orlando."

"Good thing he did, I guess," said Bert, "or we'd never have known Orlando could talk."

"I wonder if anyone else has heard the voice," said Nan.

"I doubt it," replied Dom. "Look how hard we shook him and he didn't make a sound."

Disappointed but excited, the children sat on the ledge with Orlando next to them. While they waited for rescue, the twins told Dom all that happened.

"I did not steal the puppet!" he exclaimed angrily. "I told that dopey clerk the price was too low, but he looked it up in a ledger and insisted he was right. He didn't even know silver when he saw it. I told him about the armor, but he wouldn't listen."

Bert said, "I'll bet when Mr. Wood got back and found out the mistake, the clerk got scared and blamed it on you."

"Just wait until we get out of here," said Dom

grimly, "we'll get it straightened out. And then I can give Orlando back to the Martinos. That's what I meant to do all along."

Then he told them how Tucci had brought him to the grotto in the *Red Eye*. Later Gano had come and revealed himself as Vito. "He thought that if they held me here long enough, I'd tell them the ice cream recipe. Sometimes they come in the daytime, but usually it's at night to bring me food and water."

"Do they use a torch?" asked Bert.

"Yes. They said—" Before Dom could go on there came a soft swish. The children looked up to see a rowboat filling the low entrance of the grotto.

At first it seemed to be empty but as soon as the cave mouth was passed, two figures sat up.

Vito's hoarse laugh echoed in the rocky chamber. "So now *we've* caught *you!*"

CHAPTER XVIII

THE PUPPET'S SECRET

A CRUEL grin spread over Vito's face. Tucci worked the boat closer to the rocky ledge.

The children jumped to their feet.

"No use running," said the bald man with an ugly laugh.

Suddenly Tucci thrust out an oar, pinning Dom against the wall. At the same moment Vito reached over and yanked Orlando into the boat.

Bert lunged for the puppet, but too late! The rowboat was pushed away from the side, rocking hard.

"Maybe we ought to tie 'em up," said Tucci.

"No time," the big man replied. "Besides, they can't go anywhere.

"You can forget about your friends in the motorboat," he called to the prisoners. "We saw them land at a beach about a mile and half down the coast. While the big boy climbed some wooden stairs to a cottage on the cliff top, we towed their boat away."

"The little twins were too busy playing among the rocks on the shore to notice us," added Tucci.

"What of it?" said Bert boldly. "When Peppo reached the house he telephoned the police for help. They'll have us out in no time."

Both men laughed. "I happen to know," said Tucci smoothly, "that house is empty."

"It's a deserted area," said Vito. "Your friend will be stranded a long time before he finds help."

"You might never get out," said Tucci, his voice echoing hollowly.

"Unless," put in Vito, "Dom tells me the ice cream secret."

"Don't do it, Dom," said Bert. "He wouldn't let us go, anyway."

"Don't worry," the big boy replied. "I'm not talking."

Vito scowled. "Too bad. This is your last chance. We won't be back."

When none of the children spoke, he signaled Tucci, who rowed toward the entrance.

"By the way," Vito called, "I'm going to melt Orlando's armor down for the silver." He laughed. "Then I'll chuck the puppet into Donna's kiln."

The two men ducked low, and Tucci swished the boat out of the grotto.

The children were horror-stricken. Dom

groaned. "We've got to get out of here and save Orlando!"

Bert and Nan recalled the long unbroken wall of the cliff.

"The only place we could get out of the water is the little beach," said Nan. "It's over a mile away. I don't think we could make it."

"Shh!" said Bert, sharply. "Listen!"

Faintly they heard voices calling, "Bert! Nan!"

"It's Freddie and Flossie," exclaimed Nan, "but they sound as if they're inside the earth!"

The boys and Nan made their way to the alcove, where the voices were louder.

"Here we are!" Bert shouted. "Keep calling!" He flashed the light around the walls. At the rear was a narrow opening.

"Let's try that," said Nan. "It may lead to the surface."

Bert slipped into the dark cleft, with Nan behind him and Dom last. As they wriggled upward through a tight rocky passage, the cries of the young twins became louder.

Suddenly light streamed down. A moment later Bert was looking up into Freddie's wide-eyed face.

"Give us a hand!" panted Bert, and his brother helped him crawl out. One by one the prisoners squeezed up into daylight. They were on a wide, grassy ledge of the cliff, high above the sea. From here a gentle slope led to the top.

"We saw the men steal the motorboat," said Freddie excitedly, "but we kept down behind the rocks so they wouldn't know we'd seen 'em."

"Peppo was too far up the cliff to hear us call," put in Flossie, "but we climbed to this shelf and followed the *Red Eye*."

"Good for you, Floss!" exclaimed Nan. "You and Freddie saved us!"

"We saw the two men row out of the grotto with Orlando," Freddie went on. "They took him aboard the *Red Eye*, pulled up the rowboat and went off."

"Now we've got to rescue Orlando," said Dom.

As he spoke there came a roar from the hill above.

"Motorcycles!" cried Flossie as half a dozen machines appeared in a cloud of dust.

Screeching and waving, the children raced up to the narrow road where the cyclists had stopped. Six surprised men listened as Dom breathlessly told their story.

Then the motorcycles zoomed around the mountain with the twins and Dom each clinging behind a cyclist. Near the villa they spotted Peppo, and the sixth driver picked him up.

When they finally roared into Palermo, Peppo's machine swerved off to the police station. The others drew up in front of Donna's store.

The Bobbseys leaped off and dashed through the shop into the back room.

"Give us a hand!"

"No, no!" cried Nan. "Don't do it!"

Tucci was holding open the door of the big kiln. The inside was glowing, red-hot.

"In you go!" exclaimed Vito as he shoved Orlando, feet first, toward the furnace.

Instantly Nan, Flossie, and Freddie leaped for the puppet as Bert and Dom threw themselves on Tucci. With a yell the tall man fell backward and hit his head on the floor. At the same time Vito ran for the door, straight into the arms of the five husky cyclists.

For the next fifteen minutes things were in a happy uproar. Donna rushed out from the corner where she had been watching, frightened. Peppo dashed in with six policemen who secured the prisoners. Two more officers arrived with Uncle Mario, Aunt Bartolina, Papa Martino, and Bibi.

Dom's mother sobbed for joy as she and Dom hugged one another. Papa Martino clutched the puppet.

"You found Orlando!" he said to Dom, tears in his eyes.

"And the Bobbseys saved both of us!" replied the boy.

Aunt Bartolina smothered the twins in hugs. Meanwhile the six motorcyclists shook hands all around and left.

"*Silenzio!*" shouted the police. When order was restored, Vito and Tucci sulkily confessed.

The bald man admitted eavesdropping behind

the curtain at Amato's shop. "Later I came back and listened in the alley outside the kitchen window. I heard Mario say that Dom would probably stay in Naples. So I got in touch with my friend Tucci and ordered him to pick up Dom's trail at the Naples airport."

"Where's the motorboat?" asked Peppo.

"At the waterfront," growled Vito. "We used it to bring the puppet here. Tucci's boat is in a large grotto where we kept it."

Tucci spoke up. "When Vito saw you on the plane, he knew we'd have to keep an eye on you or you might reach the boy first. After we had Dom, I followed you. I thought my trick with the car at the museum would scare you off."

"You were always in our way," Vito grumbled.

As he stared glumly at the floor, Bibi stepped forward with her black bag. "Would somebody like to buy my jar?" She pulled out a cracked clay vase. It had a small neck with a handle on each side.

Signora Donna gasped. "It's ancient Greek pottery!" As she took the vase, something rattled, and she poured out a handful of coins.

Vito's eyes widened. "Old Greek money!"

"It's no good," said Bibi. "It's all worn out."

"Why, child," said Donna, "this vase and the coins are valuable."

Vito groaned. "I could have had them for a bargain!"

"If you hadn't been too mean to talk to me," said Bibi.

As the police led the two men away, the woman returned the vase and coins to the little girl.

"They should be in the museum," Nan said, and Bibi agreed to take her treasures to Dr. Panito the next day.

Half an hour later the Bobbseys and their friends trooped into the Martinos' kitchen. Orlando was set up on a chair.

"Now tell us your stories," said Papa Martino.

"No," cried Uncle Mario, flourishing a yellow paper. "First read this cablegram. It came a few hours ago." He thrust it at Bert, who read aloud:

"CLERK CONFESSED HE MADE MISTAKE. I APOLOGIZE TO DOM AMATO AND FAMILY. SIGNED, HENRY WOOD."

"I will find out how much the puppet should have cost," said Uncle Mario, "and see that Mr. Wood gets the amount still owing."

"I feel sorry for him," said Nan, and added that if he had not accused Dom of stealing, they would not have come looking for him right away. "We might never have learned that he had been kidnapped."

Then Dom and the Bobbseys told their stories. When Nan revealed the puppet's secret, the families were astonished.

"Maybe I can fix that talk-box," said Emilio. He carried the puppet to a table backstage, and turned on a bright light. "There must be a switch under his padding somewhere."

"I thought he was wood," said Flossie.

"He is," replied Papa Martino, "under the padding. When we examined him ten years ago we didn't think to remove that." Emilio took out his pocketknife.

"Wait!" said Bert. "Try shaking him again. It might work."

Emilio lifted the puppet in his powerful arms and gave him a hard shake. There was a *click,* and then came the deep voice:

"My dear children—"

The Martinos gasped.

"Grandfather!" whispered Peppo.

"—I have a surprise for you," the cheerful voice went on. "I bought it in Milan and have hidden it in the stone chest in the ruined palace. Hurry, now." There was a chuckle and a whirring noise, then silence.

"Where's the stone chest?" asked Mama Martino.

"I know!" said Bert. "Come on!" He led the way to the palace and leaped up the stairs two at a time. The two families followed him into the room where he and Nan had found the cat.

Emilio and Vince lifted the lid off the big chest and took out a large cedar box.

"You open it, Nan," said Mama Martino.

Nan turned the key and raised the top. There was a chorus of *ohs* and *ahs*.

"Puppet costumes!" cried Flossie.

They lifted out layer after layer of silks and velvets, in glowing colors. The ladies' dresses were studded with glass jewels and the knights' doublets were decorated with gold.

"All so well packed they are just as fresh as the day Grandfather bought them," said Mama Martino, wiping tears from her eyes.

"Here's something else," said Freddie, taking an envelope from the chest. "It was under the box."

Papa Martino read the writing on the envelope. "It says, 'For new scenery and armor.'" Inside was a thick bunch of colorful Italian money.

"Oh," cried Nan, "now your theater won't have to close! Lots of people will come!"

"Thanks to you Bobbseys!" said Papa Martino.

"And Dom," chorused the Bobbseys.

"And Grandfather!" cried Peppo.

Dom's eyes sparkled. "Oh, how I'd love to work in the puppet theater!" he exclaimed.

Peppo grinned. "And I wish I had your job—making ice cream. It sounds great!"

Bert pricked up his ears. "Uncle Mario," he said, "Papa Martino—I've got an idea. Why don't you exchange boys? Then everybody'll be happy."

The two families looked amazed. Then they

laughed. "I'm for it," boomed Papa Martino, and his wife nodded.

"So am I," exclaimed Uncle Mario. The two boys whooped for joy and Della told Dom's mother, who beamed. Everyone talked happily at once, except Bibi. Her face crumpled.

"I want to go with Peppo," she sobbed.

Uncle Mario's eyes grew soft, and he put his arm around the child. "Let her come," he said to the Martinos. "I will adopt her."

"Oh, please say yes," coaxed Della.

"Do you want to go to America, Bibi?" asked Mama Martino.

"Oh yes!" the child cried and ran to Peppo. He swung her around, laughing.

"All right," said Mama Martino. "It's settled!"

As they all trooped back to the theater with the cedar box, Uncle Mario invited everyone to a party next day. "I will make my special ice cream and Peppo will help!"

"Then he'll know the secret ingredient," said Flossie.

"Yes," said Uncle Mario happily, "and because you have been such helpful children, I will tell you." He whispered into Flossie's ear: "It is specially made caramel mixed with vanilla." Smiling, Flossie told the other twins.

Next morning all the neighborhood crowded into the theater to see Orlando restored to his place of honor. The house hummed with excitement as the Bobbseys and their friends took seats on the front benches.

"Wait'll you see Orlando," said Bibi. "I helped my aunt polish his armor last night."

"And Emilio fixed the talk-box," Peppo added. He told them that it was in a hollowed-out spot in the puppet's chest. "There's a place under the padding where you wind up the device and switch it on."

As he spoke, Papa Martino stepped through the stage curtains and called for quiet.

Peppo translated softly as his father told the audience he would now present Orlando and the children who had rescued him. He beckoned to the twins and Dom, and they went onto the stage. Then Peppo pulled the curtain.

In the spotlight stood the beautiful puppet in shining armor with the children around him.

The people applauded loudly.

Then Papa Martino detached the puppet's rods and carried him down into the auditorium with the children trooping behind. As he placed Orlando in the glass case, a cheer went up.

"The King's Puppet is home at last," said Mama Martino, "and the Bobbseys learned his secret."

"They know mine, too," said Uncle Mario.

"And mine, too," cried Bibi, then clapped a hand over her mouth.

Freddie laughed. "Don't worry. We'll never tell."

Bert winked at Bibi and whispered, "But you nearly let the cat out of the bag."